THE EDEN STORIES

THE HEART OF PLUTO

TERRY TOLER

The Heart of Pluto
Published by: BeHoldings, LLC

Copyright © 2023, **BeHoldings, LLC**
Terry Toler
All rights reserved.

Book Cover: BeHoldings Publishing
Contributing Editor: Donna Toler

For information email: terry@terrytoler.com.

Our books can be purchased in bulk for promotional, educational, and business use. Please contact your bookseller or the BeHoldings Publishing Sales department at: *sales@terrytoler.com*

For booking information email: booking@terrytoler.com.

First U.S. Edition: October, 2023
Printed in the United States of America
ISBN 978-1-954710-22-1

OTHER BOOKS BY TERRY TOLER

Non-Fiction

How to Make More Than a Million Dollars
The Heart Attacked
Seven Years of Promise
Mission Possible
Marriage Made in Heaven
21 Days to Physical Healing
21 Days to Spiritual Fitness
21 Days to Divine Health
21 Days to a Great Marriage
21 Days to Financial Freedom
21 Days to Sharing Your Faith
21 Days to Mission Possible
7 Days to Emotional Freedom
Uncommon Finances
Uncommon Health
Uncommon Marriage
The Jesus Diet
Suddenly Free
Feeling Free

For more information on these books and other resources visit
terrytoler.com.

Thank you for purchasing this novel from best-selling author, Terry Toler. As an additional thank you, Terry wants to give you a free gift.

Sign up for:

Updates
New Releases
Announcements

At terrytoler.com

We'll send you an eBook, *The Book Club*, a Cliff Hangers novella, free of charge.

1

May, 2023,
San Diego, California

It felt like I was on an episode of the *Rich Working Wives* of Southern California. A popular television series that had spread around the country and featured rich women in major U.S. cities including San Diego.

Had I not been in the same situation many times over the last three years, I'd have felt extremely out of place. Considering I didn't work, and I wasn't rich.

The four ladies sitting at the outdoor dining table with me didn't meet all the criteria either. Two of them were divorced, London and Rhea, so technically, they were ex-wives. I hadn't actually watched the television show, but I heard that some of the wives on there were divorced as well.

London and Rhea were rich for sure and didn't need to work, but they had their divorce lawyers to thank for their bulging net worths and opulent lifestyles. The other two, Page and Trista, were married but weren't working wives, so they didn't fit the criteria either.

They were rich though. One thanks to her husband's billion-dollar business. The other benefited from her grandfather who started his business more than a hundred years before and passed it down to her father who grew it to a billion-dollar enterprise, then passed it on to her and her two brothers.

To say that none of the four worked wasn't really fair. London dabbled in real estate, although she rarely closed a deal and didn't work very hard at it. Rhea was an actress. So to speak. I couldn't remember the last film she was in. She didn't get major roles even when she was younger and prettier. She admitted privately that the only decent roles she got back in the day were when her husband agreed to invest in the movies. Since they were divorced, those opportunities were a thing of the past.

Trista and Page weren't working through no fault of their own. Both casualties of the pandemic. Trista owned a restaurant, which went out of business when the California governor shut down all inhouse dining because of COVID.

Page used to run a beauty boutique and day spa called *The House of Gloria*. Named after her husband's first wife of twenty years who died of breast cancer a few years before. On the rebound, he married Page and insisted she run the spa. He refused to let her change the name and she hated every minute of it.

The governor also shut down all day spas and hair salons putting them effectively out of business for more than two years. The salon eventually reopened, but Page was no longer a part of it. We didn't know the whole story.

"Do you miss the spa, Page?" I dared to ask and immediately regretted having broached the subject.

"Heavens no, Mia! You couldn't make me go back to that place if my life depended on it."

My name was Mia Cooper. I grew up with these ladies. We went to the same private school. My dad was a real estate tycoon until the crash of 2008 sent him into bankruptcy. We lost our lavish home and country club membership, but I remained friends with the girls.

When I moved back to San Diego three years ago, they welcomed me back into the clique, even though I no longer had their wealth or prestige. We had little in common now other than our upbringing, but I still loved them like sisters.

"I drove by the spa on the way to the country club for lunch and noticed it was still open," I said.

I missed the day spa where I occasionally got free massages and makeovers.

Page obviously didn't. Bringing up the subject had clearly made her angry. Steam was coming out of the top of her head. Or maybe that was the hair dye evaporating in the intense sun beating down on us.

"Who's running it?" London asked the question I was dying to know.

"His precious Amy," Page said sarcastically and in a mocking tone. "She's back from college."

Amy was one of two daughters her husband had with Gloria. She was off at college when Page married Walter. Apparently, she had graduated and taken over the family business for her father.

"She even advertises that it's under new management. Can you believe it?"

"No. I can't believe it," I said sincerely, and others voiced agreement.

All of the ladies tried to be supportive even back when Page was running it. It had to be hard for her to work in that environment. I thought so at the time. With the constant reminder of her husband's first wife, she probably never considered it her own business. It must be excruciating to be shut out now.

"Amy looks just like her mother!" Page said bitterly. "The spitting image of the picture of the younger Gloria on the wall. No wonder all the old customers are glad she's running things now."

When you first walked into the spa, the wall to the right had a massive picture of Gloria that took up the entire wall. That picture had been a huge source of angst for Page. She had complained about it incessantly.

I could see where it might be uncomfortable for Page, but I thought she made too big a deal out of it. What was wrong with her husband still loving his wife of twenty years and the mother of his children?

An opinion I never dared to voice.

It did seem odd that Walter tried to fit his square peg of a new wife into that round hole. It might've been wiser to start a new business. At least change the name and put Page's picture on the wall instead.

Gloria was stunningly beautiful, but so was Page.

"Gloria is probably laughing at me in her grave," Page said. "I never lived up to her standards with Walter."

The spa had been thriving under Gloria. Not so much under Page. Page had admitted as much at one of our previous lunches. A fact her husband reminded her of every three months when the financial statements were prepared by the accountant.

Page matched Gloria in beauty but not in personality. From what I could deduce, Gloria was extremely personable. Page was shy, not as outgoing, and a bit of a spoiled brat. From the number of cars out front today, the daughter must have her mother's business sense and personality because business was thriving again.

It was obviously bothering Page. She unloaded her pent-up frustration. She went on for a good ten minutes explaining why she couldn't stand her husband, Amy, Gloria, and that wicked spa.

It looked like Page might join the ex-wives club soon. Before long, I might be the only one married. At this point, I was obviously the only one happily married. My heart warmed as I thought about my husband, Mark, who had a big day of his own today.

"Not to change the subject," Rhea said, as she proceeded to change the subject. "You won't believe what my ex-husband did."

The other three ladies noticeably moved forward in their seats. They loved good gossip. All four were on their second glass of wine, which meant the conversation was picking up steam. I still nursed my first glass of iced tea with lemon.

"I had to pick up my daughter at school yesterday," Rhea said, her voice cracking and fighting back the tears.

Tears of anger or sadness? We'd soon know. With Rhea it could be either.

"It was quite an inconvenience. I had an audition. It was a big role. Regis couldn't get away from work."

Regis was her ex.

"So he says," she said sarcastically. "When we were married, he expected me to be at his beck and call. I was the chauffeur. Chief cook. Housekeeper."

When they were married, Rhea had a housekeeper who came every day. Still did, probably. But no reason to make the point.

Even my curiosity was piqued. It was gossip, but it's hard to turn away when a car crash is happening right in front of your eyes.

"What did Regis say when you told him you had an audition?" London asked.

Rhea raised her hand to brush back her hair which was not possible. It had so much product in it, a bulldozer couldn't move it.

"He told me to drop her off at Nevada's house."

Several of the women gasped.

"No!"

"Yes he did."

Nevada was her ex-husband's new girlfriend. Half his age. He was forty-eight, she was twenty-four. I had seen her. A swimsuit model. Also a want-to-be-actress. She was getting the opportunities Rhea used to get.

Their daughter Laney was fourteen, going on twenty-four. She looked the same age as Nevada.

5

"Nevada is not a name!" Rhea said. "It's a state. Who names their child Nevada?"

"I think Nevada is her modeling name," I said. Not knowing why I opened my big mouth.

Rhea glared at me.

"What did you do?" I asked, getting the attention off my statement as quickly as possible.

"Laney wanted to go!" Rhea said. "So I took her."

"Ohhhh," said the chorus.

We all saw the problem.

"I said no, but she begged me."

"She's only fourteen," I said. "Don't take it personally. Kids don't get caught up in all the drama like adults."

If looks could kill, I'd be a cat who had used up all her lives and died nine times right there on the spot.

"It's normal that she would like Nevada," I added. "They're closer to the same age. And you're her mother. It's not the same."

Rhea glared at me a second time, like I had said the worst thing in the world.

Somebody give me a shovel, so I can dig a deeper hole. Or a bigger mouth to insert my foot.

I couldn't leave bad enough alone. "All I'm saying is that Nevada is not that much older than Laney," I said. "She has more in common with her than she has with you."

"What does she have in common with that witch? I can't stand the gold digger."

Someone back me up here.

Someone make me shut up.

At least I was smart enough not to make the point that Rhea was a starving actress when she met her rich husband. I thought at the time that Rhea didn't love Regis. She only married him for his money. The definition of gold digger. Rhea's picture could be next to the word in the dictionary.

I'd never let those thoughts out of my mouth. I'd already said too much. The other ladies sat back in their chairs not willing to give me even moral support through body language, much less verbal agreement.

"I think it's awful," London said, taking Rhea's side. Which was what I should've done. "These men think they can trade us in for younger models. What do these girls think is going to happen when they aren't pretty anymore?"

"That's right!"

"Men are rat bags."

The waiter arrived about that moment to refill the wine glasses, thankfully getting me off the hot seat. After he left, it felt like it was someone else's turn to complain about their husband. I couldn't think of anything to say.

Thankfully, Trista jumped in.

"I've had a simply horrible week. Work is a nightmare for me," she said.

The hand to the forehead was a little over dramatic. She should've been the actress. She continued without taking a breath.

"No one's getting along. Bill is extremely unhappy, and he takes it out on me."

After her restaurant closed, Trista spent more time at the family business even though there really wasn't anything for her to do.

"I don't know what's going to happen," her voice trailed off as she said it.

"Talk to me," Page said. "What's going on with Bill?"

"As you know, when daddy died, he made Bill CEO."

We did know. It had come up many times in discussion and she didn't need to mention it again. Her two brothers had been furious.

What the brothers didn't know was that Trista had talked her father into it. She was the daddy's girl he could never say no to.

In her defense, the brothers were irresponsible. One had dropped out of college, the other had graduated by the skin of his teeth. They both had the drive of a shih tzu. More interested in fast cars, women, and partying than working hard. I didn't like them growing up and don't like them now.

While her husband wasn't as savvy as her father, he was at least able to keep the doors open and the money flowing. The medical waste disposal business had actually thrived during the pandemic for obvious reasons.

"I want to sell the business," Trista said. "If we don't, I don't think our marriage will survive."

"It's been in your family for a hundred years," London said.

"All good things must come to an end. I'm tired of all the fighting. My brothers and Bill are constantly at each other's throats."

"What does Bill want to do?"

"He thinks we should hang on to it. Pass it down to our son. That's not going to happen. Bill Jr. has no interest in the business. He wants to be a musician. He's not cut out for running a business."

"I thought business was good," I said. "Do you really want to give up the cash cow?"

Trista was the wealthiest on paper by far.

"Bill can't separate business from personal. He brings it home with him. If he has a bad day at the office, it's going to be a bad night at home. I made him a cauliflower pizza the other night. You know, I'm gluten free. He hit the ceiling."

"What did he say?" Rhea asked, sympathetically.

"He said it tasted like cardboard. That he wanted a real pizza."

Trista changed her voice to mimic her husband. Twisting her lips in the process. I hoped her caked-on makeup didn't crack from the sudden exertion.

"'I'm a billionaire,' he said. 'I can have a pizza flown in from Naples Italy if I want. I shouldn't have to eat this piece of cardboard you made. Which isn't even cooked right.'"

"What did you say?" London asked, matching her friend's disdain for her husband's behavior.

"You wouldn't be a billionaire if you hadn't married me," she said.

Trista suddenly put her hand over mouth. Like she was embarrassed she said it. She knew it was cruel. It was an extremely hurtful thing to say in the heat of the moment.

"What did Bill say?" Rhea asked.

"He said, 'Sometimes I wonder if it was worth it.'"

Trista burst into tears. I reached for a tissue in my purse. Her makeup was working overtime. First the facial distortions. Now the tears. Although, I figured the eye makeup could withstand Niagara Falls.

"That's mean," I said sincerely, as she took the tissue and dabbed at her eyes.

"What did you do next?" Page asked.

"I threw the pizza in the trash and went upstairs crying. He didn't even follow me."

"I hope you made him sleep on the couch," Rhea said.

She waved her hand dismissively. "Honey, we haven't slept in the same bed in over a year. He has his own room."

If I remembered right, their house had twenty bedrooms and even more bathrooms. They could go a year and never run into each other.

"What's going to happen to the business if you can't agree," I asked.

"We called a meeting of the board of directors. We're going to put it to a vote. I have to decide how I'm going to vote. There are four of us on the board. My two brothers, me, and Bill. My daddy did that so we would all have to get along. He figured Bill and I would always vote together and offset the two brothers. And vice versa."

"That was smart," I said. "I guess."

"I'm thinking about voting with my brothers," Trista said.

We all let out a noticeable sound of disapproval.

"I know. Bill will never forgive me."

"That's a tough decision," I said. "It's risky."

So much drama. A hard choice. Her marriage or the business?

Everyone was silent for a good two minutes. Honestly, I didn't think anyone knew what to say. It wasn't often this group was speechless.

I looked off in the distance. We overlooked the eighteenth green of the golf course. The sun was at its peak although the ocean breeze kept it pleasant. Much more pleasant than the awkwardness that had overtaken the conversation.

Eventually, it was time for someone to speak. The ladies looked at me like it was my turn to say something awful about my husband. If I didn't, I might come across as the odd cog in the wheel being held together by hatred for men.

"Mark is a great husband ninety-nine percent of the time," I blurted.

It sounded weird coming out of my mouth. That's the worst thing I could think of to say about him.

Some of the ladies were already a bit jealous of my marriage. Mark was head and shoulders better than their husbands and we all knew it. While he didn't make millions, he made a difference. Mark was a professor at a local university. Teaching science. Namely astronomy.

Page twisted her lips to the side, and I felt a snide remark coming. Page and I often clashed. She sometimes felt the need to take me down a notch. Make sure I knew she was better than me.

"Depends on what the one percent is," she said.

Her oversized duck lips flapped in the breeze as she moved them to speak. I wondered how she kissed with those things. Probably didn't.

"I suppose."

I wasn't interested in getting into an argument. Not even a discussion. It'd be a waste of time.

Page obviously wasn't going to drop it.

"If your husband was faithful to you ninety-nine days out of a hundred, would that be good enough for you?" she asked, snidely.

Her Botox fried forehead almost formed a wrinkly line when she crinkled her nose.

"I suppose not."

"What if he only beat you one out of every hundred days?"

"Page drop it!" London said. Even she realized it was an inappropriate thing to say.

I bit my lip and forced back a frown. Then dropped a bombshell into the conversation. I blurted it out before really thinking it through.

"I definitely wouldn't like getting beat up. Even if it was only one day out of a hundred. My husband does have a mistress, though."

All four ladies' eyes widened at once. Which was not easy considering all the work that had been done on them. Collectively probably thousands of dollars worth.

A sound came from the putting green below. I hadn't realized I was talking that loud.

"How long has that been going on?" Trista asked, her mouth wide open in disbelief.

Page seemed stunned and speechless for a second time. Which was the effect I wanted.

"Since Santa Cruz," I said in my most nonchalant voice.

"That's horrible."

"I've learned to accept it."

"You're okay with Mark having a mistress?" Trista asked in a shrill voice. "I'm surprised. With your Christian background all."

I was the only consistent church goer in the group.

"Nothing I can do about it," I said.

Page finally spoke up. "I wouldn't put up with it! I can tell you that for sure. You're a fool."

"You're kidding," Rhea said.

"Nope. It's true."

"What's her name?"

"Pluto."

2

University of California San Diego

Dr. Mark Cooper thought he had died and gone to heaven.

He was in his dream job. Professor at one of the most prestigious schools in America. Now one of the twelve founding faculty members of the A & A, Department of Astronomy and Astrophysics, established in March of 2023.

He had been fortunate enough to help develop the vision and was on the ground floor of building an undergraduate and graduate program that would lead the nation in research and development of the next great space adventures.

The university had a long and rich history of being in the forefront of space research, dating back to 1962, even without having a formal department. Famous faculty and staff had worked on the Hubble Telescope, numerous space missions, observatories, and the Long Wavelength Spectrometer on the Keck Telescope among other notable things.

Sally Ride was once a professor there. She was the first American woman to travel in space and the youngest astronaut ever. After leaving NASA, she became a professor of Physics at UCSD and the director of the California Space Institute, part of the nearby Scripps Institution of Oceanography.

Mark was sitting in the same classroom Sally Ride had taught in. He might be sitting in the same chair. He was in awe. It felt surreal every time he stepped foot in that classroom.

Today was the last day of the spring semester. Presentation day. Fifty percent of the students' grades were based on the papers they were required to write in place of a final exam. Five of them had been randomly chosen to present the basic gist of their paper in a one paragraph synopsis in front of the class.

The subject. The Tombaugh Regio. Pluto's heart.

The premise was simple. The students were to present a plausible theory as to what caused the heart shaped feature on Pluto.

Scientists were baffled. In fairness, the heart was a new phenomenon in science, and they hadn't had much time to study it. Such a paper wouldn't have even been possible eight years ago. Up until the year 2015, Pluto was nothing more than a blurry yellow and black blob in the far reaches of outer space.

No telescopes on earth were capable of getting a clear picture.

In 2006, NASA launched the New Horizons space observatory. Tasked with traveling to Pluto and getting the first pictures. The trip took nine years. The images took four and a half hours to send back. An amazing technological feat.

When the first images arrived on earth, the scientists were astonished. On the side of Pluto, in plain view, was a heart. An almost perfect replica of the human heart. It couldn't be more like it if it were painted on the side of the planet by an artist.

Mark was a graduate student at the time. He decided to do his doctoral thesis on Pluto. Discussing primarily the heart and Charan. The two great phenomenons of the mysterious planet.

Charan was a moon of Pluto that traveled around the planet in perfect harmony. The two bodies were gravitationally locked to each other. Constantly facing each other.

Like two lovers in a kissing contest.

How could they be so perfectly aligned?

By the time Mark finished the thesis, he was hooked on the dwarf planet. Obsessed with Pluto was a better word. If he could, he'd spend every waking moment studying it.

His thesis was well received, and he earned his doctorate from the University of California Santa Cruz. The number one ranked school in America for physical science research. He finished at the top of his class and was offered a professorship right away.

When the opportunity arose three years ago to take the same position at University of California San Diego, he jumped at the chance. His wife, Mia, was from there and they both loved San Diego more than Santa Cruz.

Mark was from Oklahoma. In spite of his Midwest, Bible belt, Judeo Christian worldview, he had found a way to fit in. Mostly because the students loved him, and his humorous off-the-cuff teaching style was a hit.

Not all of the faculty loved him. Some only tolerated him. They didn't like his teaching style, which was considered unconventional.

One of the conditions of his employment was that he could continue a class he had started at UC Santa Cruz. The Marriage of Regio. A class that studied Pluto. More specifically, Tombaugh Regio. The formal name of the heart.

A play of words on the opera, Figaro.

Mark preferred the informal name, Sputnik Planitia, because informal fit with his teaching style. The Marriage of Regio fit his humor better.

Mia had actually named the class back in Santa Cruz. They were joking about the heart of Pluto one night. As they often did. His obsession with the planet. Their marriage.

"Whose heart do you love more?" Mia had said. "Mine or Pluto's?"

"You're jealous."

"You are married to Regio," she said in a mocking British accent. Something she often did.

That's when she blurted out the Marriage of Regio and the name stuck.

Several of the faculty thought the name was undignified for a Physics class. Beneath the seriousness of scientific research. Astrophysics was considered a serious medium and should be met with strict decorum.

"It's a boring medium," Mark had argued, before he was hired. Even risking not getting the job. Which was fine. He was happy at Santa Cruz.

"Physics is not boring for me," he said when pressed, "but for most students it is at first. We need to make it less tedious for them. Let's make physics fun."

The decision makers extended him an offer. They really wanted him. He had excelled as a professor at Santa Cruz and had impressive references and academic achievement.

It was a good match. The students loved his classes and he had won over most of the faculty. They couldn't argue with the results. Mark had managed to make a subject as boring as Pluto fun for the students.

None of the other professors had a waiting list of students wanting to take their classes.

Mark stood from his chair and called the class to attention.

"Last day," Mark said.

Everyone groaned. Mark doubted any of his colleagues got that same reaction. It warmed his heart.

"When I call your name, come to the front of the class and tell us what you think caused the Cosmic Valentine."

Another one of Mia's clever names. She had several as it related to the heart of Pluto. Some he couldn't share with the class. Those were of a more intimate nature. Banter best left in the privacy of their bedroom.

Mark tried to put that out of his mind. He had a class to teach, and Mia was distracting him even though she was miles away having lunch with her hoity toity country club girlfriends she grew up with.

He focused back on the task at hand and said, after too long a pause, "If you say aliens caused the heart, then you'll get an automatic F." He had a huge smile on his face when he said it, so they'd know he was kidding. He got the expected laugh.

He wasn't exactly kidding. Someone did write that in a paper once. He would've given the person an F except that the thesis was well researched and written. The student got a C instead.

Mark looked down at his list of students selected to make the presentations. He had put the names in a bowl and Mia drew them out the night before.

"Rashmi Muni," Mark said.

The class murmured then began cheering him on. Mark didn't mind. He didn't care if another class heard them having fun. Good advertising for his class.

Rashmi was well liked by the other students. Probably because he was one of the brightest minds in the school. Not just the Physics department. He was a former national spelling bee champion and had an IQ of 170.

Mark had him in other classes as well and was shocked when he signed up for this one. As were other members of the faculty who thought the class was beneath his skill level. Mark thought the class was just what someone like Rashmi needed. Something to challenge him.

The best minds in the world hadn't solved the heart matter. Those students who really tackled the problem were forced to learn a lot about physics, physical science, and any number of other topics. Depending on how they did their research.

Rashmi held a piece of paper in his hand and began reading his theory. "Underneath the heart of Pluto is an ocean of liquid nitrogen. The nitrogen rises to the surface and freezes. Forming the heart."

Mark wanted to groan. Rashmi was taking the safe route. The traditional view.

"What causes it to freeze?" Mark asked.

"The temperature on the surface of Pluto is 248 degrees Celsius."

"You mean *minus* 248 degrees Celsius," Mark said. Rashmi was nervous.

"Right."

"What is that in Fahrenheit?"

Mark could see him doing the calculation in his head.

"382 degrees Fahrenheit below zero."

"That's correct. What about when Pluto is closest to the sun? Sometimes its orbit takes it closer than Neptune's. Wouldn't the Nitrogen ice melt and evaporate?"

"It probably does. To some extent. But the ocean underneath gives it a steady supply of nitrogen that refreezes."

Mark asked him a few more questions which Rashmi answered with the standard information he had studied in books. Mark would've preferred his students think outside the box a little more than that, but he could hardly penalize him for presenting the most logical explanation.

"Thank you, Rashmi."

The class applauded as he took a bow and returned to his seat.

Mark didn't need to look down at the paper. One of his favorite students was next. A senior from Germany. A bright and outspoken serious minded blonde. She was graduating in a few days. This was probably her last class.

"Elsabeth Biermann."

The class cheered. She walked confidently to the front. They continued cheering and she turned from nervous to embarrassed when Mark mentioned she was graduating soon with honors.

"Rashmi is wrong," she said, when the din died down.

"Oh!" the class responded raucously. Mark winced at the noise. They might be having too much fun.

He did like the opening. When students challenged each other. He encouraged it. If they had time, he'd let Rashmi and Elsabeth debate the difference. Whatever it was. The class might learn something. Unfortunately, they didn't have a lot of time.

"I think what's underneath the surface is water not nitrogen," she said. "The water freezes and glaziers form at the surface. Like it does on earth in Greenland, Antarctica, and the North Pole."

"If it is water," Rashmi said, "wouldn't the ice gravitate toward the equator and form a belt?"

"The glaziers do move," Elsabeth retorted. "We see them change positions on the ice in the pictures. Like glaciers move on earth."

The exchange between the two continued for a few minutes. Both presented well thought out arguments.

"How deep is the ocean?" Mark eventually asked.

"It's two and a half miles deep."

She had answered immediately, which was what he wanted to see, but he would've preferred a less definitive answer. She spewed out what she had read. He had taught his students to question everything. That's what science did.

The leading experts said with certainty that the basin was two and half miles deep. How could they possibly know without examining it? Without sending a submarine to the bottom and measuring it?

Kind of like scientists who said with certainty that the earth was 4.5 billion years old. The actual equation was 4.54 Œ 109 years ś 1%.

Whatever.

How did they know? Those same experts didn't even know how old their wives were. How many years they'd been married. Or where they parked their car after a San Diego Padres baseball game.

A soapbox Mark wasn't going to get on today.

"Thank you, Elsabeth. Time to move on. Congratulations on graduating. I'm proud of you."

A broad smile came on her face. It's the closest she had ever come to beaming around him. She should be proud. A degree in Physics from UCSD was not an easy task.

"The next student to present is Mo Wen."

Mo Wen was from China. His demeanor was always as serious as a cancer diagnosis. Mark had never seen him smile. He didn't have the IQ of Rashmi or the ability to apply critical thinking like Elsabeth, but he was an extremely hard worker.

He rarely spoke unless spoken to. Mark was glad his name was drawn. This would be good for him.

More whistling, hooting, and hollering from the class. The noise level kept increasing with each student. Mark silenced them. They were getting too loud. It's one thing for another class to hear them, another to disturb them.

"Rashmi and Elsabeth are both wrong," Mo said with a grin.

Mark felt a smile come on his own face.

"The heart is a combination of methane, nitrogen, and carbon dioxide trapped in a basin," he said.

"Why do you think it's a basin?" Mark asked.

"It's the only thing that makes sense. Pluto doesn't have a strong gravitational pull. When gasses come to the surface anywhere else on the planet, they go into the atmosphere. They don't in this region. That's because it's a low-lying area. Like a basin."

He paused to see if Mark wanted to respond.

"Go on."

This theory was well known to Mark. There probably wasn't a theory out there he hadn't studied in detail. No student had come up with something he hadn't heard before.

"The gasses can't escape to the atmosphere within the heart because they are trapped in the basin. They freeze before they can escape."

Mark asked him a few questions and then let him sit down. Mo seemed relieved when he walked back to his chair.

"Next up is Clarissa."

She began speaking before she even got to the front of the class.

"With all due respect to my colleagues, they are all partially right and all partially wrong."

The noise ratcheted up again. The class began to needle Elsabeth, Rashmi, and Mo.

"Please explain," Mark said.

"It's not a basin, it's a crater. Caused by space rocks crashing into the surface of Pluto."

Another common theory.

"Why do you think that?"

"The top of the heart is consistent with the circular outline of a meteorite," Clarissa said. "I believe more than one hit Pluto. Perhaps thousands."

"There are thousands of planets and moons in the solar system," Mark said. "Is there anything even remotely similar? Wouldn't we see heart shapes on other planets?"

"The Caloris Basin on Mercury is similar in some ways. Of course, Mercury is closer to the sun so it's silicon based. Not ice based."

Mark was impressed. At least she had done her research. Not that he was surprised.

He asked her a few more questions but time was running low, and he wanted to get to the last presenter.

"Thank you, Clarissa."

The class applauded dutifully. They also heeded his admonition to hold it down some.

"Our last presenter is Lee Barrett."

Lee made his way to the front. When he turned and faced the crowd, he had a huge grin on his face.

"The heart of Pluto was caused by aliens," he said.

Everyone roared laughing. Including Mark. That was funny.

"I'm writing down an F," Mark said, pretending to write on the paper.

"I'm playing. Here's my theory. Like Clarissa, I considered meteorites, but I rejected that idea. Rather than meteorites hitting the planet creating a crater, it's the other way around. The crater was caused by a volcanic explosion."

Mark had hoped someone would take that position. It's something he had seriously considered. He was glad all five presenters had taken a different approach. That made it more interesting for him and his students.

"The eruption blew out the side of Pluto. Lava rose to the surface. Most escaped into outer space. The rest froze on the surface."

Lee paused waiting for a question or response from one of the other students. When none came, he continued.

"Pluto is in the Kuiper Belt, which is full of debris. I believe the unusual amount of debris in the area is from the volcanic eruption."

"What's your theory on what fills the crater?" Rashmi asked. "Who is right? Elsabeth, Mo, or me?"

"I don't know," Leo said. "Any of you could be right. I don't think that's the important question."

"Isn't that the purpose of the exercise?" Mark said. "To come up with plausible theories as to what formed the heart shape?"

"Actually, it's not."

"I'm the one who set the assignment. I think I would know."

"I'm not trying to be argumentative, professor, but everyone is focusing on the wrong thing."

"Enlighten us."

Another breath. Lee's hand was shaking.

"I mean no disrespect, but my four fellow classmates have given you several different theories. Their presentations were researched and well thought out, but I think they failed to focus on the heart of the assignment. Pun intended."

He waited for the light chuckling to subside. Mark wasn't amused.

"The assignment was to explain the heart of Pluto," Mark said.

"My fellow colleagues are making an assumption that there is a scientific explanation for the heart."

Mark was starting to get frustrated.

"There is a scientific explanation. That's the point of the assignment."

"You should ask a different question," Lee said.

"What question is that?" Mark said roughly.

"How is it possible?"

"How is what possible? You aren't making sense."

"Maybe the heart was formed by nitrogen. Maybe it's methane. Maybe it's a combination. Maybe there's an ocean of water underneath. Whatever. The question we should all ask is how any of those things could come together to form a perfectly shaped heart. No one in any of their presentations has attempted to explain it."

"Then why don't you explain it to us."

"I intend to. The heart of Pluto was formed by God," he said emphatically and with authority.

The class gasped. Then they booed. Mark held his hands out to silence them.

"Let him finish."

"The heart is a sign," Lee said. "Like the rainbow on earth. God gave us the rainbow as a sign that he'd never destroy earth again with a flood."

Mark was shocked. Religion was rarely, if ever, mentioned in a science class at a liberal university. If it was mentioned, it was only to ridicule the ideas.

Mark had heard the story of the flood in the Bible many times. He believed it as a child but hadn't thought about it in a lot of years. While he was a man of faith and believed in God, there was also scientific evidence for a flood. So he believed it did happen.

The Ark and Noah were a little far fetched.

"Something happened on Pluto," Lee said. "Something catastrophic. Maybe a volcanic explosion. Maybe a nuclear explosion. Maybe a meteor. Who knows? I think whatever it was destroyed all life on Pluto. The heart didn't form by accident. It's a sign to us. I don't know what that sign means, but it's a message to us from God."

Mark's heart began to race.

He was stunned.

A student had finally come up with a unique theory. Something he had never considered.

This was one of the most remarkable things he had ever heard in his life.

3

3:00 A.M.

I woke from a deep sleep in a sweat even though it was cool in our house. This time of year, the normal low was a chilly fifty-five degrees in San Diego.

I sat straight up in bed. It took a few seconds to get my bearings. Something was wrong. I looked to my right. The clock beside my bed said it was the middle of the night. Three in the morning. Normally, a sound sleeper, I couldn't remember the last time I'd been awake that early.

I turned to the left. Toward the bathroom. My eyes didn't need to adjust to the darkness because the bathroom light was on. I'd left it on for my husband Mark. He'd called me earlier that evening and said he'd be working late.

"Don't wait up for me, Mia," he said. "I'm on a roll with something."

That was the second call. The first call was around five. He said he'd be a few hours late. That wasn't unusual. Especially at the end of the year. He probably had papers to grade or grades to post online. He didn't say.

Mark always had his grades ready to turn in early. Before anyone else. Today was the last day of class. Perhaps he was trying to get them in *really* early.

To shake away the cobwebs, I shook my head from side to side.

Mia wake up.

Why?

What was wrong?

I instinctively reached for Mark's side of the bed. As I often did to rustle him when he snored. I'm not sure why I did it this time. I could clearly see he wasn't there. The sheets and comforter were untouched.

What?

I looked at the clock again. I couldn't believe it. Not only was Mark not in bed, he hadn't been there at all.

Am I dreaming?

It seemed real.

"Mark," I called out, thinking he might be in the bathroom. Hearing my own voice told me it wasn't a dream.

He didn't answer.

A wave of panic came over me, causing my whole body to shake. Completely overcoming the drowsiness.

I told myself not to panic. He was probably downstairs working on the home computer. I slipped out of bed and went into the bathroom just in case he was in there. He wasn't.

I looked at myself in the mirror. Wiped the sleep from my eyes and mussed with my hair out of habit. Inspected the countertop for any sign that Mark had been there recently.

No sign that he'd been in the bathroom since yesterday morning. Not that I could necessarily tell. Mark's side of the double vanity was always perfect. Everything in its place. My side was messier.

When it came to beauty products, I was a bit of a hoarder. Was always trying the latest and newest thing. Which would be fine, except I never threw anything away. Half-used bottles of all kinds of enhancers surrounded my sink. Most of which I'd never use again but couldn't make myself get rid of.

Most of the products were a waste of money. I usually reverted back to a more natural and understated look. Which Mark preferred and I liked better compared to the layers of makeup on my friends at lunch the day before.

I left the bedroom to continue my search for my husband. Trying to remain calm. The house was two stories and I stopped at the landing on the top of the stairs and peered over the banister.

Why?

What was I afraid of?

The downstairs lights were still on. I'd left those on for Mark as well. It appeared nothing was different from when I came to bed.

"Mark," I said, louder this time. No response. I walked slowly down the stairs.

Why was I walking so cautiously? Like a character in a Hitchcock movie. An unsuspecting victim about to be attacked by an intruder. It's silly. We lived in a safe gated neighborhood. I had no reason to feel fear.

Yet I did.

The lights cast my form into an eerie shadow on the wall which added to the trepidation. My imagination was running wild. My hands clutched the railing and I was fully prepared to bolt back up the stairs at the first sign of danger.

Not sure where I would hide upstairs. Maybe lock myself in the bathroom or cower in the closet. If someone wanted to get to me, they could. We didn't have a safe room or a gun.

Halfway down the stairs, I stopped and leaned over the railing again so I could see the entire living room and kitchen which were one room.

"Stop being paranoid," I muttered to myself when I didn't see anything. "He's probably in his office. He'd better be."

Mark's office was in the back of the house next to the spare bedroom. The hall lights were off, so I stopped before walking that way. The lights off meant he wasn't there. No reason to even check.

After looking on the couch to make sure he wasn't lying on it, I walked to the kitchen and propped my elbows on the oversized island. Thinking.

What's going on? Where's my husband?

My mind replayed the conversation from the night before. I vaguely remembered him mentioning his class. That something exciting had happened and he couldn't wait to tell me about it.

It didn't fully register and I didn't think anything of it at the time. When Mark talked about school, astronomy, or physics, he was always excited. His voice usually had a slight sense of urgency to it when he was talking about his favorite subject.

Talk to him about the latest beauty product I purchased at the store on sale and his eyes glazed over. He listened dutifully but didn't offer any of the excitement he showed when talking about his work.

Especially his mistress. Pluto.

The thought made me giggle out loud.

My mind wandered to the lunch with my girlfriends. I shouldn't have said that to them but couldn't help myself. Every one of them about came out of their false eye lashes when I mentioned the word "mistress." Now that I thought about it, I shouldn't have said it for another reason. They'd all probably dealt with their husbands having one or more women on the side at one time or another.

The thought of Mark being with an actual mistress popped into my mind. I quickly dismissed it. That was ridiculous.

Why was I nervous though?

Duh.

It was three in the morning and my dependable clockwork husband wasn't home. Any normal person would be freaked out. Even more than I was.

I called out his name again but wasn't surprised when he didn't answer. The house wasn't so big he wouldn't hear me the first two times I did it.

"Mark, it's Mia. Are you here?" I said, practically shouting this time.

I'm not sure why I mentioned my name.

Maybe he's working in his office. On his computer with the lights off.

Why didn't he answer me when I called his name from the hallway?

It wouldn't be the first time he had tuned me out. That was in the one percent of things annoying about him. There were times when Mark would look right at me while I was talking and it seemed like he didn't hear a word I said.

When he was obsessed with a project, I could walk in his office naked with bells around my neck and red flashing lights on the top of my head and he might not notice. I'd mentioned that to him on more than one occasion. He didn't think that was true and kept daring me to try it.

I probably shouldn't have said to the ladies that Mark was great ninety-nine percent of the time. I had been bragging but couldn't help myself. Those ladies were always boasting about how much money they had, the trips they took or were taking. Showing off their new clothes or new car or new house or new boyfriend or new piece of jewelry.

They made me feel inadequate.

Not that I cared about things. I had nice things growing up, but after my dad's business failed, and especially after I married Mark, my lifestyle took a hit.

So what. I really was happy with Mark. I wouldn't trade my life with any of those ladies. He was the best thing in my life. I meant it every time I said it. He was great ninety-nine percent of the time. It wasn't an exaggeration.

I'm not so happy with him at the moment, though.

Depending on his explanation about tonight's blip in the marriage radar, I might have to lower the percentage. This was distressing. He'd better have a good reason as to why he wasn't in this house.

Maybe he's sleeping in the guest room and didn't want to wake me.

I went back to the hallway and flipped on the light intent on doing a more thorough search. I walked with a purpose toward the guest room, certain I was right.

I called out his name again, so he'd know I was coming and not to startle him or awaken him from a deep sleep.

That'd serve him right.

No answer.

That didn't stop me from checking the room. Even looking in the bathroom and closet.

No sign of him. I even turned on the office lights and checked the closet. Not at all sure why he would be in the closet, but I checked anyway.

The angst returned with a vengeance. Bordering on panic. I still had more places to check though.

The next place was the garage. I walked back to the kitchen and through the mudroom. I flipped on the light and opened the door to the garage. My car was there, but Mark's parking spot was empty.

My heart sank.

I wasn't sure why I expected it to be there. He wasn't in the house. Why would his car be there?

Up until now, I'd been able to control the panic rising inside of me. Not seeing his car unleashed a range of emotions. Anger to fear, annoyance to dread. Each emotion escalated the more I thought about it.

I closed the door slowly.

"Where are you, Mark? You'd better be lying in a ditch some-where," I said aloud.

The comment made me chuckle nervously. We'd talked about the figurative ditch many times. It was always him mentioning it. Mark was the overprotective one. Any time I left the house, he'd tell me to call when I got to my destination.

"Mark, I'm just going to a ladies Bible study. It's five minutes from here."

"I know. But it'll be dark soon. It'll definitely be dark when you're leaving. Let me know when you're heading this way. If you aren't home in ten minutes, I'll send out the posse."

He was so annoying sometimes.

"I'll be fine," I had argued.

"I need to know that you aren't lying in a ditch somewhere."

"Where are these ditches you're always talking about? I grew up in San Diego and I haven't seen any ditches."

"San Diego has ditches."

We brokered a compromise. I'd send him a text when I arrived at my destination. The problem was that I kept forgetting. He'd end up calling me when I didn't report in on time. His calls inevitably came at an inopportune time. Interrupting whatever I was doing.

My hands might be full of produce on the grocery store aisle and I'd have to fumble in my purse to find my phone. The call might come during the opening prayer of the Bible study. He'd always insisted I leave the phone on. Putting it on silent was okay, as long as I kept the vibration feature activated.

A vibrating pocket or purse was almost as disruptive as a ringtone. One time, I forgot to call him and didn't hear the vibration from the phone buried deep in my purse. Maybe I heard it but ignored it. Either way, he showed up a few minutes later. To make sure I was okay.

That was the final straw. He needed to chill out. After a huge argu-ment, we finally agreed to put a location tracker on our phones. If he wanted to know where I was, he could find me at any time as long as my phone was on, which I promised to always be diligent about.

Things were going well until the time I forgot to charge my phone and the battery went dead and he couldn't find me on the location app. He was so mad, I thought he was going to have an aneurysm when I got home. That led to one of our biggest arguments.

"If you see me on the app in a ditch, you can come find me," I had joked to ease the tension between us and put an end to the argument.

"It's not funny. I love you. I can't stand the thought of living life without you."

Tears had welled up in his eyes when he said it. He was genuinely hurt. It warmed my heart to see that side of him. Over the next few weeks, Mark started pointing out all the ditches in San Diego which was funny at first. After a while, it became annoying as well. As did the whole smothering act.

But things could be worse. He could be one of those husbands who didn't care where I was. That's the main reason I had accepted the obsessive behavior.

"I love you, too," I said. "I don't want to live without you either. But you need to trust God. He'll protect me."

Which was why I couldn't let myself freak out now. The conversation reminded me to stay calm. I didn't want to turn into a crazy woman and find Mark asleep in the guest room or sitting on the back porch looking at the stars.

The back porch!

It made me realize I hadn't searched everywhere. The back porch was a good idea. Maybe he couldn't sleep and was sitting outside.

He wasn't there.

It was a beautiful evening. The stars were out. The chill in the air was refreshing. The full moon had brightened the sky. I didn't rush back inside. I said a quick prayer on the back deck and a peace came over me.

Check your phone, I heard the Holy Spirit say in a still small voice.

Of course.

Now I was glad I had agreed to the location app. I could solve this mystery immediately. It meant I had to go back upstairs. My phone was plugged into the charger on the nightstand next to our bed.

I was kicking myself for not checking it right away. That's the first thing I should've done. My hand shook as I pulled up the app on the phone. Trying to remember how to use it. I rarely used the location app. Knowing Mark, he used it all the time.

It showed a blue dot at our house.

What? That's impossible.

"That blue dot is your phone, dummy," I realized.

Scrolling down, I found the word PEOPLE. Mark was the only person in my shared file. I clicked on it and waited for his blue dot to appear.

Relief washed over me. Mark was still at school. I wasn't sure why that made me feel better. He could be dead in his office or lying in a ditch at school. Mugged on his way to his car.

I frantically searched my phone to see if Mark had called me. Texted. Emailed. Anything. Surely if he was going to be this late, he would let me know.

Nothing.

The peace I felt on the back porch was gone. I reminded myself to stay calm. He was probably still working. That's the most logical explanation. For whatever reason, he forgot to call me and let me know he'd be this late. Or maybe he didn't want to wake me up.

I could hear the conversation in my head.

"Why didn't you call me?"

"I did call. Twice. I told you I'd be late."

Now I was angry. And wide awake. What did he think I'd think when I woke up and he wasn't there? He'd never been out this late before. Ever. Of course I'd be worried. Who wouldn't be?

What if the tables were turned and I was the one out this late? He'd have a hissy fit. He got upset if I was five minutes late getting home from the gym.

I angrily found his contact on my phone and called his cell phone.

If he's not dead, he will be when I get a hold of him.

Don't even joke about it. It's not funny.

4

Mark answered on the first ring. My heart skipped a beat when I heard his voice.

Now that I knew he was alive, I could focus on why I was angry with him.

"Where are you?" I asked, roughly.

"I'm sorry, Mia. I'm still at the office."

"Do you know what time it is?"

He hesitated.

"I'm guessing it's close to midnight."

"It's three in the morning!"

"Oh."

"What are you doing?" I demanded to know.

"I told you I'd be working late," he said defensively.

"You didn't say you were going to be out all night! I woke up and you weren't here. I was worried."

"I lost track of time."

"What's so important that you have to stay at the office until all hours of the night?"

"I'm working on a new Pluto theory."

"At three in the morning!"

I don't think I'd ever been this mad at him.

"It's a promising theory. I can't wait to tell you about it."

I ignored the sincere tone in his voice. He wasn't going to sweet talk his way out of this one.

"You couldn't pick up the phone and call me? Or send me a text? Let me know you're still alive?"

"I'm sorry."

Tears had welled up in my eyes. I fought them back.

On the one hand, I was relieved to the point of being overjoyed that he was okay. On the other hand, I wanted to wring his neck. What made it worse was that he didn't seem the least bit concerned about my feelings. He was acting like it was no big deal.

"I'm sorry" wasn't going to cut it.

"When are you coming home?" I asked. Softening the tone somewhat, so I didn't come across as obsessive as he often did.

"I don't know. I'm kind of in the middle of something."

I let out an angry sigh. "I'm going back to bed."

"Good idea. I'll be home soon. I promise."

"Stay as long as you want. I don't care."

"I love you."

"Yeah. Me, too."

I hung up, immediately regretting the tone. I felt so guilty, I sent him a text with a heart and bright red lips in the form of a kiss and the words, *I love you. I'm glad you're still alive.*

I meant it. We promised each other we'd never go to bed angry and never had.

Did this count?

When I crawled into bed, that's the first thought that popped into my head. I was still mad. If he wasn't there and in the bed with me, were we technically going to bed angry?

The argument sounded stupid. *I was going to bed and I was angry.* That's the literal meaning of going to bed angry. No amount of rationalization would change the truth.

Neither would justification. Who wouldn't feel angry in my situation? This was not acceptable behavior for a married man. Not that I thought he was with another woman. It's just inconsiderate to stay out at all hours of the night and especially not communicate where you were to your spouse.

How was I supposed to sleep now?

If I didn't go to sleep was I technically going to bed angry?

The Bible actually said not to let the sun go down on your anger.

The sun was already down. Can I stay angry until sundown tomorrow?

The thoughts were making my head hurt. Maybe it was the crash I felt coming caused by the spike in adrenaline at three in the morning.

At least Mark was okay, I kept reminding myself. For an hour, I tossed and turned in the bed. A couple of times, I thought about getting up.

If I'm not in bed, then no one can say I'm going to bed angry.

I rejected that thought as well. I didn't want to be awake when he got home. An argument in the middle of the night when we were both tired was not a good idea.

We rarely fought. It had been months since we'd said a harsh word to each other. Maybe more than a year. The fight that led to the location app, might've been the last time we had what I would consider a blowup. And even that was mild compared to some of the knock down drag out fights the ladies at the lunch talked about almost every time we got together.

More tossing and turning kept the anger close to the surface. A range of emotions were making it impossible to sleep. To make matters worse, I felt like a hypocrite. I'd made such a big deal about him wanting to know where I was at all times, now I was doing the same thing.

Was it the same?

Why was it okay for him to be mad at me if I didn't call?

Not calling when I got to the grocery store was a lot different than not calling at three in the morning.

I could hear his arguments.

"I did call you. Twice."

He called me and told me he'd be late. Even called a second time when it was going to be later than he thought.

I needed to have my rebuttal arguments ready.

"I've never been out past ten o'clock at night."

"I was working."

"If I ever was for whatever reason, I know I'd have the courtesy to call and let you know."

"My work is important."

"And I'm not?"

"That's not what I meant."

"If the shoe were on the other foot, you'd be furious."

"No I wouldn't."

"If it had been me out until three in the morning without an explanation, every policeman in the county would be looking for me."

I had no doubt that was true. That was my best argument. How would he feel? Mark wouldn't be as patient as I think I've been.

I finally drifted off. At least I think so. It wasn't a deep sleep because I was awakened by a sound coming from downstairs. The garage door opened. Then closed. A minute or so later, the door to the mudroom opened. I strained to listen. It was shut too quietly to hear from upstairs.

The refrigerator door opened. I heard him pour something in a glass. Then heard the familiar sound of crackling, a power bar wrapper. Loud enough to hear all the way upstairs. I envisioned him devouring it.

He probably didn't have dinner.

Serves him right.

It wasn't my fault. I cooked dinner for him. Put it away in the fridge after the second call. I left a note for him. Telling him to warm it up when he got home. He obviously ignored it.

I looked over at the clock. *Five a.m.*

What the heck?

My husband had basically stayed out all night.

I heard footsteps on the stairs.

I quickly laid my head on the pillow and pretended to be asleep. I lay motionless in the bed. Pulled the covers more tightly around my head so they almost covered my face. I squeezed my eyes tightly shut.

The footsteps stopped and he hovered over the bed. I could feel his presence. Could even hear him breathing which made me realize I was holding my breath.

He went into the bathroom a few seconds later and washed off his face. Brushed his teeth. Gargled with mouthwash.

Mark was obsessive about having good breath. When he was home, he brushed at least half a dozen times a day. Always kept an abundant supply of mints in the house and at his office. The first thing he did in the morning and the last thing he did at night was obsess about his dental hygiene.

Now that I thought about it, worrying about my location wasn't the only thing he was weird about. Mark was obsessive about a lot of things. I already knew that about him, but it was becoming more prominent in my mind. This was something I was going to have to live with.

Thankfully, this was the first time something like this had happened.

And it had better be the last time.

He finally flipped off the bathroom light and slipped into bed. Careful not to disturb me. I was glad he didn't try to kiss me. I didn't want him to and I had my own morning breath that would knock over a mule.

As much as I hated to admit it, it felt good to have him home.

He fell asleep right away. I could tell by his breathing. Even that made me mad. I was wide awake. He was the one asleep. And all this was his fault.

I did doze off because I woke up in another sweat. This time from a nightmare. I dreamed I woke up and Mark wasn't home. I searched the bathroom and then downstairs.

I went outside. His car wasn't in the driveway. Strange since we had a garage and that's where we kept the cars. That's how I knew it was a dream.

It wasn't our house. I checked the location app and he wasn't at work. I couldn't find him anywhere. He didn't answer his phone or respond to texts.

I called the hospitals. Then the police.

Suddenly, I was running. Through our neighborhood.

I found him lying in a ditch.

That's when I woke up.

It took a second for me to realize I was awake. I looked at the clock. *Seven a. m.* The sun peeked through the curtains. I looked at Mark's side of the bed and was relieved to see him lying there, not in a ditch.

I reached over and touched his shoulder. He didn't even stir.

It was reassuring. He was in bed. It had been a dream.

That part of it anyway. I suddenly remembered why I was mad at him. The other events of the night did happen. He really was out until five in the morning.

I would confront him about it when he woke up.

For now, I needed to get some coffee in me. Do something to shake the ominous feeling that was still eating at my soul. For some reason, I still felt anxious. A feeling of impending doom hovered over me like a dark rain cloud.

It felt like something was still wrong. Like something bad was about to happen. We'd dodged a bullet the night before, but that didn't mean we would in the future.

I fumbled with the coffee maker. It had been months since I actually made coffee. Mark always got up before me and made it to perfection. Just like I liked it.

When it was ready, I poured a cup and went on the back porch to enjoy the beautiful morning and try to calm down. A slight chill was in the air, even though summer was just around the corner. I had on long pajamas and a long sleeve sweatshirt with thick socks on my feet. Without the coffee I would've been too cold to sit out there.

About an hour later and after several more cups of brew, the door opened and Mark appeared with his own cup of coffee in his hand. He kissed me on the forehead.

I smiled. Both from the warm gesture and because I could smell the mouthwash he left in the air. Which I thought was funny. How did he drink coffee with the minty taste in his mouth? That'd ruin it for me.

Did you sleep well? I wanted to ask sarcastically but resisted the urge.

A passive aggressive approach wasn't my style. I was direct. If I wanted to say something, I said it. Mark was a peacemaker. He avoided a confrontation like he avoided a root canal.

If left up to him, he wouldn't even mention last night. His approach would be to pretend it never happened. Hope I didn't bring it up.

Fat chance of that.

He took a sip of his coffee and let out an approving moan. The coffee wasn't nearly as good as when he made it. If he noticed, he didn't say anything.

In fact, nothing was said for three or four minutes.

What's up with that?

He sat across from me in the wicker chair, staring off the porch. Like he was deep in thought. Was he thinking about his project? Had he even given me a second thought?

Is he going to say anything?

The awkward silence was making me mad again. Sitting on the porch waiting for him to get up, I'd been talking to God. Convicted that I needed to forgive him and drop it. It made me feel better. Not as mad.

I could forgive him but wasn't going to let it go. I deserved an explanation. Surely he knew that. I'd made the same arguments to God.

"Were you with your mistress last night?" I finally said.

Mark laughed. Then frowned. He didn't make eye contact with me, which was weird. He knew I was upset.

"If I was with a mistress until five in the morning, I don't think I would've bothered coming home."

"I told the ladies at lunch yesterday, that you had a mistress. I was right."

He laughed again, this time more nervously.

"You did not tell them that."

"Yes I did."

"I told you I was working on something. I was at school the whole time."

"With your mistress."

He chuckled again. "Well ... I'd like to meet this woman. If I'm going to be accused of having a woman on the side, I'd at least like to know who she is and what she looks like. Is she pretty?"

"I told them Pluto was your mistress."

He burst out laughing.

"Are you saying I'm gay?"

"No! Why would you ask that?"

"Pluto is a man."

"No it's not. The planets are female."

"They are not. They're male. Technically, they're inanimate objects. Actually ... inanimate matter, to be more precise."

His eyebrows furrowed. I sensed a science lesson coming.

He changed to his teaching voice confirming it. "Inanimate matter can grow, reproduce, consume, and die. Planets can do all those things. Inanimate objects can't."

He looked at me for the first time. I glared at him. He looked away.

"Anyway, planets are neither male nor female," he said.

"Mother Earth."

He nodded. "Good point. You're right. The Earth and its moon are considered feminine. The rest of the planets are masculine in name and in imagery. They are named after male Roman gods."

"What about Venus? She's a girl."

He rubbed his eyes roughly. "I forgot about Venus. I'm still half asleep. You're right again. She's a Roman goddess."

You'd think one of the world's foremost experts on astronomy would know that. Even if half asleep.

I didn't say anything. I might be mad, but I wasn't mean. Mocking him didn't seem like a good idea. We were at least having a civil discussion. It hadn't evolved to fighting. I'd try not to let it descend to that level.

I wasn't in the mood for science lectures though.

"Pluto is definitely a man," he said.

"No, it's not."

"Yes it is. I think I'd know."

"You didn't know Venus was a woman."

"Yes I did. I forgot. I didn't get much sleep last night."

And whose fault is that?

My girlfriends would never hear about this argument. They'd think the whole discussion was stupid. As the conversation was unfolding, I was beginning to think they were right.

"Have you ever seen the dog, Pluto?" Mark said. "The one in the cartoons? Definitely a male."

I vaguely remembered. I didn't watch much television growing up.

"I've never thought about whether Pluto the dog was a male or female," I said, in an indifferent tone.

"Technically, he's anthropomorphic."

I rolled my eyes at him even though he didn't see it unless it was out of the corner of his eye. Being married to a professor had its drawbacks. This was one of them.

"What does that word mean?" I said, humoring him. He was avoiding a confrontation. Maybe I was as well.

"It's an animal who takes on human characteristics."

"Like Donald Duck?"

"Precisely. Another male."

"Actually, you can't tell by looking at him. He doesn't have anything down there, if you know what I mean."

"Then why does he cover himself with a towel?" Mark had a wide grin on his face when he said it.

I fought back a laugh. How was I going to let him know I was mad at him if I played along with the banter? I'd already let him derail the conversation I intended to have with him. The one that had played out a dozen times in my head. In my mind, it had never gone this direction. Talking about cartoon characters' private parts. Or lack thereof.

"That's a good point," I said. "He doesn't need a towel."

I really wanted this inane topic of conversation to end.

He must've sensed the same thing. "How did we get on this topic?" he asked.

"We were talking about your mistress, and you changed the subject. On purpose."

"Oh right. Pluto. My so-called mistress. Definitely a man."

He had a point. I didn't know any females named Pluto, but I wasn't ready to cede the argument. I didn't know any males named Pluto either.

He continued, before I had a chance to think of a persuasive argument.

"Pluto has always been considered a male figure in pop culture and in science," he opined. "Take Pluto on Popeye."

His lips twisted to the side. "Actually, Popeye is binary."

"Wasn't the character's name Bluto? Not Pluto."

"I think it's Pluto."

"I think you're wrong."

"Maybe."

"Like you're wrong about Pluto being a man."

"I think I would know. Do you remember what I do for a living?"

"That's right. You're the foremost expert in the world on planets."

"Right."

"You have an IQ of 155."

"Yep. Although I think it's higher. I was sick the day I took the test."

"But you aren't smart enough to pick up the phone and call your wife."

"Touche. I figured you were going to bring that up at some point."

"I think I deserve an explanation."

He changed the subject. Which infuriated me.

"Jupiter, Saturn, Mars, Venus, and Mercury were all named first," he said. "Because they were discovered first. Before telescopes were invented."

Do I look like I care? Was he really that oblivious to reality?

"Jupiter was named for the king of the Roman gods. Venus is the goddess of love and beauty."

"See. Venus is a woman."

"Not really a woman. Feminine designation is how I would refer to her."

Whatever.

I really didn't care.

"Uranus and Neptune were discovered later. Originally, Uranus was going to be called Georgium Sidus. After King George the whatever. The third or fourth I think."

Someone put me out of my misery,

"They should've named it George. Anything would be better than Uranus."

How did I let him suck me into this conversation?

"Do you want to know how all the planets were named?"

"Not particularly."

He ignored me. "Mars was named after the god of war."

"That's definitely a male. Only men start wars."

"Yep. And because of its red color."

"Women wear red."

"Neptune was going to be called Le Verrier. After the man who discovered it. But eventually they named it Neptune. Because of its blue color. Neptune is the Roman god of the sea. A male."

"Women wear blue. I bet the planets were named by men."

"Yes they were."

"They should've let us name them. We could've done a lot better. What does the name Pluto mean?"

He paused. Then frowned. Tapped his palm on his forehead like he'd just made a great discovery.

"What?" I asked.

"Pluto is named after the god of the underworld!"

"Satan?"

"Yes. I should've thought about that last night."

A chill went down my spine.

Not only was Pluto a man but named after the evil one.

I am definitely going to have to quit calling Pluto his mistress.

5

The conversation moved inside when both of our coffee cups were empty. I was cold anyway and Mark still hadn't given me an explanation for his horrendous behavior the night before.

He mentioned he was hungry. For some unknown reason, I blurted out, "I'll fix us breakfast."

Immediately feeling stupid. Why would I fix his breakfast? After what he put me through. Do you give a dog a treat after he pees in your house instead of outside in the yard?

Of course not.

Maybe if he'd shown the least bit of remorse. He'd apologized a dozen times. But that didn't cut it. Was he really sorry? It didn't seem like it.

I had a knife in my hand aggressively cutting the mushrooms and tomatoes for the omelet. Taking out my aggression on the poor vegetables.

An omelet!

I should be making him two runny undercooked eggs. Served with burnt toast.

Someone should give me a wife-of-the-year award.

He tried to be helpful and set the table. For the most part, neither of us said anything. I focused on cooking, and he disappeared into his office after the table was set.

By the time the breakfast was ready, the anger was mostly gone. The Bible was right. Nothing like serving someone to accelerate forgiveness. The verses were in the forefront of my mind. I'd heard them since I was a child.

Love your enemies.

If a brother asks for a shirt, give him a coat.

Or something like that. I wasn't that proficient in Bible verses. My parents weren't particularly religious. I was drawn to and loved going to church as a child. For some reason. In spite of their lack of interest.

I don't remember not loving God.

My salvation formally came at age fourteen and that's when I was baptized. Not long after, I fell back into my old habits. I had my circle of rich girlfriends who didn't have anything to do with God. They drew me back into their superficial lifestyles.

None of them went to church. I still did, but they had more influence on my behavior than the church did.

Once I moved away to college and met Mark, I found my faith again. He was from the Midwest Bible belt and was much more proficient in the Bible than I was. He taught me a lot and got me back into church.

Even then, we weren't what I would consider all in. We attended regularly but kept our distance. More because of Mark than me. His job was problematic. It shouldn't be but was. Religion was looked down upon at his liberal college. At best, tolerated. At worst, denigrated and even persecuted.

It's not that he would lose his job, but he wasn't willing to test the invisible boundaries. He could easily get canceled if he became too vocal.

So our spiritual life suffered. I'd like to be more involved in our church but had accepted our situation.

I did know enough to know that I had to forgive him. Even if he wasn't completely remorseful and forthcoming with an explanation.

At that point, what did it matter? It is what it is, as the stupid saying goes. Regardless, I was glad the anger was gone. Out to sea like a piece of driftwood in San Diego harbor.

Besides, I knew the explanation.

Mark was obsessed with two things in this world. Pluto and my body. He loved both of us intensely. He didn't know how to moderate his behavior with either of us.

Last night, Pluto was his obsession. Most nights, it was me. Mark was good about leaving his work at the office. When he was home, I was his focus. That's what made last night so maddening. I wasn't used to not having him home. Hundreds of consecutive wonderful nights together should offset the one night where things went off the rails.

At least that's what I kept telling myself.

I could press for an explanation, but the reason he was out late was apparent and simple. Something about class yesterday triggered something in him. He got immersed in it and lost track of time.

What I needed to do was make sure he knew it could never happen again. He may have already gotten that message by my demeanor. If not, I'd make sure he knew how I felt. One way or the other. Even if he didn't bring it up. I would. In a loving manner.

Speak the truth in love, was a verse I remembered.

Mark let out an approving moan when he finished his last bite of omelet. I was pleased with myself. He might be smarter, but I was the bigger person. I had made the first peace gesture.

My relaxed demeanor was hopefully enough to let him know I wasn't going to chop his head off if he told me about last night. Actually, all I needed to do was get him talking about Pluto.

"What happened in class yesterday?" I asked, in the most gentle and sincere tone I could muster. With no hint of vitriol behind the question.

"The most amazing thing," he said, while wiping his mouth with a napkin.

He stood and picked up the dishes to carry them to the sink.

Was that it?

Was that going to be the extent of his explanation?

I wasn't about to let him get away with it. Fortunately, the anger didn't come back. It could have. My heart was still soft toward him. Forgiveness was still in place, although the "forgive seventy times seven" verse popped into my mind. I may have to go through the process of forgiving him again, if he walked out of the kitchen, upstairs to brush his teeth.

Which was the first thing he usually did after eating. If he came downstairs and was planning on going back to school, I might lose it again. Stewing all day until he came home was not something I could let happen.

"Just put the dishes in the sink," I said. "I'll take care of them."

I didn't want him distracted.

"Okay. I'm going to pour another cup of coffee. Do you want one?"

"I'm good. Thanks."

I'd already had four or five. I'd lost count. My hands were already shaking, and I had the energy of a triathlete. I also wanted to go upstairs and brush my teeth. I had the breath of a triathlete after finishing the race with a twenty-six-mile marathon.

"Let's go back outside," he said. "The sun's out and it's warmer. I can tell you about my class."

A good sign that he wasn't going to rush off to school.

"I'll meet you out there," I said. "I'm going to use the restroom first."

To scrub my teeth. I sensed we were about to make up. He'd want to kiss me if we did. I didn't want to send him to the emergency room.

He went out the door to the back porch and I went upstairs to freshen up. I felt better when I joined him on the back deck. Genuinely excited to know what he was so excited about.

It was nice outside. The temperature had warmed to about seventy-two. I touched Mark's shoulder when I walked by. Displaying enough warmth to let him know I wasn't furious anymore. It wasn't with as much warmth as he'd come to expect from me, but would send the exact message I wanted to send at that moment.

"It's a beautiful morning," he said.

"First day of summer," I replied.

"Technically, the first day of summer isn't until June 21."

"Summer solstice."

"June solstice, if you want to be exact."

Why does he do that?

"First day of winter in the southern hemisphere is on June 21."

I resisted flashing him an annoying frown.

"I always think of summer as the first day that you have no more classes until the fall," I explained. We were getting off on the wrong foot in this discussion.

"That makes sense."

"Tell me about your class."

"It's incredible."

"I'm excited to hear about it."

He had no idea how excited I was. I hoped it wasn't a letdown.

"You know I always do the Heart of Pluto papers on the last day of class. I pick five students to make a presentation."

"I know. I picked the names out of the hat."

"Right."

Mark always had to start at the beginning. Fill in the backstory, even if I already knew it. I was used to it.

"One of my student's, Lee Barrett, presented an interesting theory I'd never heard before."

Another science lesson was coming. Mark was about to go into something way over my head. Over the years he had probably explained every possible theory to me. I knew them better than most. It would be interesting to hear the new one and my curiosity was piqued.

"He said the heart was formed by God."

I almost fell out of my chair. Not what I was expecting.

"Formed by God?"

"Yes. He said it was a sign. Like the rainbow on earth."

"That's interesting."

"I know! I spent half the night researching it. I looked up all the verses on the rainbow. God destroyed the earth with a flood, but he saved Noah and the ark."

"I'm familiar with the story."

"Of course. The rainbow was a sign."

"More of a promise really. That God would never destroy the earth again with a flood."

"Right. Lee's theory was that God formed the heart on Pluto as a sign as well."

"A sign or a promise?"

"I don't know."

"Why does he think it's from God?"

"Because the heart is so perfectly shaped that it couldn't be by coincidence."

I let out a moan of agreement. "I've always thought that. That things don't happen by chance."

"Me too."

It warmed my heart when he agreed with me. That was my love language. It especially meant a lot to me when Mark agreed with me. Probably because he was so smart.

"I've always believed that God was behind everything in the universe," I said.

"I believe that too, but I've never factored God into science."

"Why not? If there is a God, which there is, why wouldn't he be the creator of science?"

"Exactly! Lee's presentation got me thinking. I've always kept God separate from my studies. I realized last night that I might be making a big mistake."

"I see God in everything."

"I believed that in my heart, but not in my mind. Last night has totally changed how I look at science."

"How so?"

He stared away deep in thought. "Let me give you an example. Last month, researchers in Illinois released a paper. They published it in the Physical Review Letters."

Mark was sitting forward in his chair. He sat his coffee cup on the table beside him and began talking with his hands. He'd come to life. He was excited. Practically giddy.

That's what happened last night. He was so excited he couldn't think about anything else. Not sleep. Not dinner. Not even me.

I remembered that was one of the things I fell in love with at the beginning. His passion. For me and for his work.

It might be hard for him to display the same passion for both at the same time. That's why he was out until five in the morning and hadn't given me a second thought.

He continued. "Have you ever heard of muons?"

I shook my head.

"Muons are subatomic particles."

"Okay."

Not that I knew what subatomic particles were, other than I figured they were small.

"They are similar to electrons but heavier."

If they were that small, I wondered how they weighed them. I decided to keep quiet, so the conversation stayed on its current trajectory.

Mark was opening up. With no pretense. Things were back to normal between us and I liked it.

"Muons have a negative charge to them. They're created when cosmic rays collide with particles in our atmosphere."

None of it made sense, but I would have to put up with the explanation like a long bad joke to get to the punch line."

"I got it," I said. "They were researching muons."

"Conducting experiments. They studied how muons moved through a magnetic field at nearly the speed of light."

He glanced over at me. Did he see my eyes glazing over? I tried to consciously wipe the dumb look off my face. I didn't need the context. He did though.

"The point is that muons have an internal magnet that causes them to wobble," he explained. "They're like electrons in that way."

"I didn't know muons wobbled."

I didn't know what muons were. Much less that they wobbled. But it sounded good to throw that sentence into the conversation.

"What's so significant about the wobble?"

His face lit up like the lights on a Christmas tree.

"Get this! The researchers shot beams of muons into a magnetic storage ring. Doughnut shaped. About fifty feet in diameter. The temperature in the ring was minus 450 degrees."

"That's cold."

"Yes it is. Guess what happened."

"How can I guess? I have no idea."

"The speed of the wobble varied! Isn't that remarkable?"

"Yeah. It is," I said, trying to match his enthusiasm. With not the slightest clue as to why it was remarkable.

"What's remarkable about it is that it was not predicted," he said, as if he sensed my confusion.

Rather sensed my ignorance.

"Why is that remarkable?" I at least knew the right questions to ask.

"It means the muons were affected by a mysterious factor."

"Hm. What is the mysterious factor?"

"That's the whole point. We don't know. Up until now, the consensus was that there are four forces of nature."

"Only four? What are they?"

"Gravity. Electromagnetism. Nuclear force, which is the strongest. That's what holds the nucleus together. The fourth is a weak force that causes decay."

I was starting to get it. Maybe.

"So there's a fifth force?"

"There has to be. Another force is causing the muons to wobble in a way that the other four forces could not have caused."

"That's fascinating."

I meant it.

"Like dark matter."

"Yes!" he said, pointing at me. "Just like dark matter. Another thing we can't explain. Some force out there is affecting matter. We've not been able to identify it. Dark matter is another thing we can't explain. We know it's there, but we don't know what's behind it."

"Is it the same force affecting the muons?"

"Maybe."

"Did the researchers come to any conclusions?"

"The study just came out. I was reading it the other day. I looked at it again last night. The only conclusion was that there is a fifth force. No doubt about it."

"What if that fifth force is God?" I asked.

"It might be. That's what has me intrigued."

"How does this relate to Pluto?"

"I don't know. But Lee's presentation got me thinking about it. Maybe we are making a big mistake. We approach scientific experiments and theories based on what we can prove. That's why we never consider God in the equations."

"God needs to be the first thing you think about."

"Yeah. I'm beginning to see that. I never considered the God factor when I thought about what caused the heart shape on Pluto."

"Okay. So if you do add God into the equation, how does that change what you think about the heart on Pluto?"

"What if God was the one who formed it? Intentionally."

"That'd be incredible."

"It wouldn't change what we do as scientists. There'd still be a scientific explanation for it. God works within the element of science."

"Of course. God is behind the creation of everything in the world, including science."

"There's no other phenomenon in the universe like the Tombaugh Regio. The heart is unique."

He waited for me to respond, but I deferred. He was on a roll. I wanted him to finish his thoughts. My heart was leaping around in my chest, doing cartwheels like a gymnast. I'd seen him excited about science many times. This was the first time I'd seen him excited about God.

"The heart is unique to Pluto. That can't be an accident."

"I agree. I don't think a heart would form like that by coincidence. What are the odds?"

"I need to calculate them. I started that equation last night. I was in the middle of it when you called me."

"I'm sorry."

I'm not sure why I apologized. When we started this conversation, it was me demanding an apology. I certainly wasn't sorry at the time. It seemed ironic that I might've interrupted my husband when he was on the verge of a scientific breakthrough.

He waved his hand dismissively. "No reason to apologize."

I agree.

"Think about it, Mia. There's a scientific explanation for the heart. It might be caused by water under the surface freezing. The heart might be in a basin or a crater. Whatever. The point is that it forms a perfect heart. How is that possible unless God is behind it?"

"And you think he was giving us a sign."

"That's what I thought at first."

"But you don't now?"

"No. Why would God be giving us a sign? What does Earth have to do with Pluto?"

"I don't know."

"God already gave us our sign. The rainbow."

"What if he was giving Pluto a sign?"

"That's what I'm saying."

I felt my mouth drop open.

"Are you saying that maybe there was once life on Pluto?"

"Maybe."

"If you could prove that it'd be huge."

"I know! What if a catastrophe happened? Like the flood on earth. And God gave them a sign."

"Or a promise?"

"Exactly. I've long believed that the excessive amounts of debris near Pluto was from Pluto. What if something happened and the planet was destroyed? The side was blown out."

"An explosion?"

"Maybe."

"What kind of explosion would cause a debris field that big?"

"A nuclear explosion comes to mind. But it could be anything. A meteor could've crashed into the side of Pluto. A volcano could've erupted causing it to explode from within. Regardless, something happened to create the huge crater that blew out the side of Pluto."

"If there were people on the planet, it would've been catastrophic. No telling how many people lost their lives."

"I know."

"The heart was given as a promise. Their rainbow."

"Maybe."

"A promise that he'd never destroy Pluto in that way again."

I looked at him with pride. Not anger.

I could see why that might keep my husband up all night.

6

Two years later

The meeting of the peer review panel was scheduled for the first week after spring break. Mark had anticipated that day for nearly two years. Mia had been living under the pressure of it for two years as well.

Mark wrote an article called *The Heart of Pluto: An Alternative Formation Theory*. Based on the premise that God formed the image. He'd conducted research for two years while maintaining his other duties and submitted the article to the Dean of the Astronomy and Astrophysics Department for a peer review, as he was required to do.

Today he'd learn if they approved the publication of the article or if all his work had been in vain. At least as far as presenting the theory to the scientific community. Mark wouldn't trade the last two years for anything. It'd been the most invigorating and satisfying accomplishment of his career. Even if no one else knew it.

Mia certainly did. She couldn't have been more supportive.

"Whatever they decide, I want you to know I'm proud of you," she said to him, before sending him off to what felt like the proverbial wolves. He didn't like having his fate in the hands of others. Not when it came to something this important.

"If they say no, the last two years of effort would be for naught."

He regretted the words as soon as they came out of his mouth. She shook her head.

"It won't be for nothing," she articulated, what he knew to be true. "Think of all you've learned. Not to mention how much you have grown in your Christian faith. It's brought both of us closer to God."

He nodded. "That might be the very thing that derails the article."

The article would be controversial. Heresy to some in the scientific community who didn't believe God had a place in the discussion.

Mark would see how much of a hornet's nest he had stirred up when he met with the peer review board later that morning.

Normally, an article was submitted directly to a scientific journal. The journal editors would select scientists in the field to scrutinize the work and make recommendations. Called a peer review. The journal would then make a decision, to publish or not to publish, primarily based on that review.

That's not how it worked at the University of California, San Diego. Mark wasn't allowed to submit his work outside of the university without their approval. It had to be submitted to the dean of his department, who would conduct her own peer review. Standard operating procedure for all of the university's faculty and staff.

Their way of controlling what came out of the university. Articles were considered a reflection of the university as well as the person who authored them. This applied to books as well. It was part of Mark's employment agreement, so he had no other choice.

The director, Dr. Cecilia Steele, normally chose three members of the faculty or former faculty of the university to review the work and make a recommendation on publication. In this case, she chose herself as one of the members. They'd had the article in their possession for more than three months and would render their verdict today.

If the board approved, they'd consult with Mark and choose the best journal for publication. The journal wouldn't be allowed to conduct its own peer review. They had to accept the internal review of the university if they wanted the opportunity to publish the work. If they didn't, a dozen others would relish the chance.

As such, the university chose what articles were published in the scientific journals from their school, and not the other way around.

If the board rejected his article, it was buried and never heard from again. The only way to get it published would be to quit. Something Mark was not prepared to do. He loved his job. One of the most distinguished professors, at the most prestigious department of astronomy in the world.

"I want it for the kids as much as myself," Mark said, nervously. "They worked so hard."

"Yes they did. You all deserve this."

Five students helped Mark with the research, including Lee Barrett. The student who first devised the theory that God was behind the heart. Mark chose four other students from diverse backgrounds. Various religions including one atheist. He thought that would add to the credibility of the paper.

Turned out, the young woman ended up giving her heart to Christ through the process. She got down on one knee in his office and he led her to the Lord. She eventually became one of the theory's biggest advocates.

"You worked hard, Mark," Mia said. "I'm proud of you."

"So did you. You put up with so many late nights."

"I didn't mind."

After the late-night fiasco two years before, Mark agreed not to stay out past Mia's bedtime. He was always home before she went to bed. If he lost track of time, she called him. If he wanted to continue with his work, he did so in his office at home. Which he did many times.

Mark looked over at her with deep admiration. He'd never been more in love with her. They'd grown closer over the two years. Like Mia said, they'd grown closer to God which brought them closer together.

They rarely missed a Sunday of church. They joined a life group and developed other couples as friends. Mia spent less time with her country club girlfriends, only joining them occasionally for lunch. While his workload was doubled by the article, he made more quality time with Mia and their relationship hadn't suffered.

He'd be devastated if the board rejected his article. He was so sure he was right about his theory. Or at least on the right track.

Mia walked over to him and motioned for him to scoot his chair out from the table. She sat on his lap and put her arms around his neck. He smelled a hint of lavender from the shampoo emanating from her still drying hair.

She must've sensed his nervousness.

"Be anxious for nothing," she said, quoting the familiar verse and adding another. "God causes all things to work together for good. Remember that. Either way. Regardless of what happens."

"I will."

"They're going to love it."

"Always the optimistic one."

"I don't know any other way to be."

"I'm a scientist. I'm trained to be a skeptic. To question everything. The board is made up of other fellow scientists. They're trained in the same way. To view everything through a questioning lens. To see if it withstands scrutiny. My views are pretty far out there."

"3.1 billion miles to be exact," she said with a wide grin on her face.

"I'm impressed," Mark said. "You know exactly how far Pluto is from earth."

"I've been over that article as many times as you have. I could make your presentation to the board."

"Why don't you? You can go in my place."

"Oh no. I think I'll stick with doing the dishes. They're less stressful."

He looked down at his watch. "I'd better go."

He left but not before they shared several intense kisses along with more words of affirmation from Mia. By the time he got into his car, he was ready to take on the world.

That's what Proverbs 31 meant. A husband was respected in the marketplace because of his wife. The world version was "behind every good man was a better woman."

Either of those sayings applied to him and he felt extremely lucky to have Mia in his corner. He wouldn't want to face this level of scrutiny alone. Anyone who dared to venture into writing an article for a scientific journal, had to have a thick skin. Criticism came with the territory. He could take it. It felt good to know that if he was rejected, he'd be coming home to her.

He expected the criticism to come in bushels today. Which was fine, as long as they agreed to publish. This information was so important, he had to get it out there. It could change the way astronomers looked at other planets forever. In his mind, if proven, this would be the most important scientific discovery of the twenty-first century.

Prolonging the torture, Mark had to teach a class first before the meeting. He barely remembered what he said. He wondered if anything made any sense to his students. His mind was on the peer review meeting. It couldn't come soon enough.

The students were dismissed, and Mark went to the vending machine to get something to quench his parched throat. He ended up choosing plain water. Sugar and caffeine would increase the nervousness. Which was already at high levels. If a doctor took his blood pressure at that moment, he might admit him to the hospital immediately.

Mark gulped down the water, packed his things, and walked the short distance to the administrative building of the Astronomy and Astrophysics Department. Arriving early. The meeting was to be held in the conference room. The three members of the review board were already present and seated with his article and notes sitting on the table in front of them.

Dr. Cecilia Steele motioned for him to take a seat on the empty side of the table. Dr. Byron Ogley and Dr. Duan Zhu sat on the other side. The greetings were warm but professional. Mark hadn't been particularly pleased by the choice of peers. He had other faculty members he preferred more. He also had some he preferred less, so he counted his blessings. It could've been a lot worse.

Dr. Steele led the discussion. She was clearly in charge. Her demeanor matched her name. Her hair was bound so tight on the top of her head, it looked like it would hurt her scalp. Her business suit was accented by a thin black tie that matched the ties worn by all the men in the room.

He couldn't wait to hear her critique. Dr. Steele was a flaming liberal politically. A poster child for women's rights and the Me-Too movement. He didn't know her religious affiliation. If she even had one.

"We have reviewed your work," Dr. Steele began. Her eyes on the notes in front of her. "Thank you, Dr. Cooper, for the opportunity to consider the article for publication. I can tell that you are passionate about it and put a lot of effort into it."

"Thank you."

"I must add that we all found it interesting."

That could be a good or a bad thing.

"I found it more troubling than interesting," Dr. Zhu said, peering over his wire rimmed glasses.

Mark knew he'd be the biggest critic. The vote didn't have to be unanimous. A majority would rule the day. Mark only had to convince two of them. Even if they were inclined to vote no, he still had time to change their minds if any of them were on the fence.

On the other hand, Mark was well aware that the decision to publish might already have been made and there was nothing he could do to change their minds. Even if that were the case, they'd wait to hit him between the eyes with the verdict. They'd make him squirm for a while and wonder.

It also might be possible that they would provide tentative approval. Based on Mark making changes. Some things he wouldn't compromise on.

Mia had wisely reminded him to go into the meeting with an open mind. Not defensive. Confident. Bold even.

"What did you find troubling, Dr. Zhu?" Mark asked, feeling calmer and with resolve building.

"Are we running a school of theology or a science department?" he asked, derisively, looking at Dr. Steele when he said it.

She frowned.

"We are running a science department," she said.

"I am well aware of that fact," Mark said, with boldness. "That doesn't mean we shouldn't consider the spiritual dynamic when it intersects with science. As it does in this case."

"You have no proof that the fifth force of nature is God," Dr. Zhu said. "The muon experiments are inconclusive."

"That's correct. We are making an assumption in the article."

"A rather far-fetched one, if you ask me."

Mark immediately responded. "The article presents a theory. All theories are based on assumptions until proven. If the things in the article were a fact, then I wouldn't have called it a theory."

Dr. Ogley spoke up for the first time. He'd be the most sympathetic to the argument. If he was adversarial, Mark would know he had an uphill battle on his hands.

"I found the whole premise preposterous," he said.

Mark's heart sank.

Then he wondered. Was he playing the devil's advocate? Scientists often shielded their real beliefs in order to force other scientists to articulate and support their theories.

Mark took a deep breath and reminded himself to stay calm. "Which part?" he asked, calmly.

"All of it. I'm confused. Was the crater that formed the heart made by God or by man?"

"Both. I'm saying that a nuclear explosion formed the crater. God was behind making it into the shape of a heart."

"And your theory is that Pluto once sustained life."

"It certainly had the potential to. We can clearly see water from the images."

"And the people who lived on Pluto blew themselves up. Some kind of nuclear explosion."

"That's the theory."

"With no basis of fact to support it."

"It can easily be proved."

"I wouldn't say easily," Dr. Steele interjected.

"I'll cede the point," Mark said. "Pluto is 3.1 billion miles away. It's not like we can take a car and start conducting experiments."

Dr. Steele nodded. "That's precisely my point. The New Horizons probe ended on September 30, 2024."

"I know."

"A new probe would have to be commissioned."

Mark began to speak excitedly.

"But think of the scientific possibilities. A new probe could land on Pluto and collect samples within the heart and in other parts of Pluto. It could continue on to the Kuiper Belt where it could collect debris samples. We would compare the samples from the debris to see if it came from Pluto. If it did, that'd prove one element of my theory. That much of the debris in the Kuiper Belt was caused by an explosion on Pluto."

"Which you think was caused by some kind of nuclear explosion," Dr. Zhu said with a hint of disgust in his tone.

"Correct."

"A nuclear war?"

"That's right."

Dr. Zhu let out a sound of disgust. "Perhaps you should write science fiction novels instead of scientific papers."

Dr. Steele raised her hand to interrupt. The meeting was going off the rails. Mark was starting to get angry as was Dr. Zhu. Mark could see it in his clenched jaw and glaring looks. He tried to control his own body language.

"I personally thought the article was well-written and well researched," Dr. Steele said. "Even if it is unrealistic."

"What part is unrealistic?"

"You can never prove it. Not in the near future anyway. The cost to build and launch New Horizons was roughly 750 million dollars. It cost 14.5 million dollars a year to manage it for nineteen years. It'd probably cost twice that now. I don't see any way you're going to get funding for this project."

"I disagree," Mark said. "This theory could prove life on other planets. When have we ever had that opportunity before?"

"It won't prove anything," Dr. Zhu said.

"Let him finish," Dr. Steele said.

"If the debris in the Kuiper Belt came from Pluto, then it means that the heart was caused by an explosion."

"An explosion that could've been from a volcano or meteor crashing into it," Dr. Zhu said. "Likely one of those two."

Mark shook his head.

"My team looked at that. It'd take thousands of meteors to form a crater large enough to form the heart. Talk about unrealistic and far-fetched. My team rejected that theory. A volcano wouldn't blow out that big an area either."

"Neither would a nuclear explosion," Dr. Zhu said.

"Maybe not. But a nuclear war might."

"Like I said, go write science fiction novels. You can call it the *War of the Worlds*. Oh. That's right. It's already been written."

Mark was undeterred. "If the debris in the Kuiper Belt contains nuclear material, and it came from Pluto it would confirm my theory."

"If, if, if, if. Dr. Steele is right. No one's going to spend a billion dollars on ifs."

"We do it all the time. Why did we spend a billion dollars to send New Horizons to Pluto in the first place? To explore the unknowns. Isn't that what we do here? We're all fascinated by space because of what little we know. I think there was once life on Pluto. A catastrophic war destroyed the planet. Maybe I'm right, maybe I'm wrong. This mission might keep our world from going down the same path."

"It's interesting," Dr. Ogley said, "I'll give you that. But I think the article would've been better if you had left God out of it. That was unnecessary. But I understand why it's there."

"The article will get people talking. I know it'll be controversial. That won't be the first article published that was. It also wouldn't be the first published that was totally out of left field. But this article is vital. If for no other reason, then to get people thinking about our own planet. And what nuclear war could do to us. Think of the debris field earth could cause if a nuclear war occurs."

"I can see that," Dr. Ogley said.

"It's one theory. Our team had to settle on one or we wouldn't have an article."

"Why did you have to put God in it?" Dr. Steele said.

"As scientists, why can't we consider every possible theory? Why do we have to limit our discussion to only the physical realm that we can see, feel, and touch? Why not at least consider the spiritual dimension?"

"Because we deal with scientific theory and proofs," Dr. Zhu said. "Based on assumptions. God does not exist. Therefore, that assumption discredits the entire paper."

"With all due respect, that might be your view, but it's not mine and it's not the view of the students who helped me with the project."

"Why are you involving students in a study of religion?" Dr. Zhu said.

"They volunteered for the study and were given class credits."

"That's another thing. Why are we giving credit hours for studying God?"

"Dr. Steele approved the class credits."

"I didn't know about the God angle," she said. "I wouldn't have approved it had I known that's what the article would be about."

"We didn't know that's where the paper was heading until we got into it," Mark said. "Science leads to where the facts lead."

Dr. Zhu threw the paper on the table in disgust. "This article is a pile of rubbish. I will never approve it."

"Your vote is registered," Dr. Steele said. "How about you, Dr. Ogley?"

He got a pensive look on his face.

"I vote yes," he said, causing Mark's heart to leap with joy. "I don't think it hurts to have a spiritual dimension to a paper and let people decide. That leaves you, Dr. Steele. What is your vote?"

"I actually like the article. A lot. It's very well written and the research is thoroughly documented. The whole idea that the Kuiper Belt debris might be caused by an explosion on Pluto is fascinating. I don't know that anyone has ever considered that possibility before now. It's something that deserves exploring. While I doubt we could get funding for such an ambitious project, considering New Horizons just went to the Kuiper Belt and Mars seems to be the focus of everyone's attention, I think it is worth pursuing."

She's going to vote yes!

"Based on that I would vote yes. With one caveat."

"What's that?" Mark asked.

"That you take out all the references to God and focus only on the nuclear explosion and life on Pluto angle."

His heart sank to the bottom of his chest. "I can't do that."

"Then I vote no." She closed the folder in front of her. "Thank you, Mark, for the article, but we are not going to approve it for publication."

"Then I resign my position!" he said, angrily. "I'll finish out my term. Then I'm done."

"As you wish."

Dr. Zhu seemed gleeful.

Mark stood and stormed out of the room.

7

Eight weeks later

Mark had been borderline depressed ever since the peer review board rejected his article and he impulsively quit. I'd done everything I knew how to do over the last eight weeks to try to get his spirits up. The doldrums intensified the closer we got to the end of the school year and Mark's dream job was coming to an end.

"I can't believe tomorrow is my last day," Mark said, despondently.

I expected this and had planned a nice evening. I'd ordered his favorite pizza and was wearing his favorite short shorts. Discussing his last day had been avoided until now.

"I know," I answered. "Hard to believe the school year is over."

"Tomorrow is my last day at UC, San Diego."

As if I didn't know. I'd been dreading this day since he came home and told me he quit. I knew how he felt. I still couldn't believe it.

"It's surreal," I said.

"Look at you, Mia, using big words."

"I know a few."

He abruptly stood to his feet and disappeared down the hallway to his office. He returned with a bowl in his hand. I didn't see him take it out of the kitchen cabinet, but I thought I knew what it was for.

In the bowl were small pieces of paper, confirming I was right.

"Time to draw five names out of a hat," he said. "Tomorrow is Marriage of Rigio day. Heart of Pluto presentations. The fate of my students are in your hands. If they only knew."

"Too bad they don't know," I said. "Some of them would probably pay me money not to draw their names."

The five names meant nothing to me, but Mark seemed excited.

"You did good," he said. "These are good choices."

"I didn't really *choose* them."

"I know. It's random. I like your picks though. Two years ago, you drew Lee Barrett's name," he said. "Do you remember?"

"How could I forget?"

"Ironic isn't it? How different our lives would be if you hadn't pulled his name out of that hat. I'd still have my job."

"So it's my fault!"

I knew he was kidding and smiled widely so he knew I was as well.

His face became despondent again.

"No, it's definitely my fault. I'm the one who quit."

"I'm glad I chose Lee's name," I said, trying to keep him from going into that pit. "It's changed both of our lives. For the better. That article is amazing. Someday it'll be published."

"I doubt it."

"You'll see. When are you going to learn that I'm always right?"

"I hope so. But the university owns the rights."

That had been a wrinkle that came out of nowhere. Mark quit so he could publish his article at another school. Turned out the fine print of his employment contract stated that the university owned all rights to articles and studies conducted while under their employ. Mark couldn't publish the article without their permission, which they'd never give, even if he found someone to publish it.

We went to an attorney to see if we could do anything about it. His words were sobering. The contract was ironclad. While the article was intellectual property and Mark had certain rights to it, the research was done on school property. With school resources.

"I did a lot of the work at home," Mark had said. "Mia can confirm it."

"The contract is clear," the attorney said. "If an article is written during your tenure at the school, the publication rights belong to the university. If you try to publish it yourself, they'll sue you. And they'll win."

"I'll sue them for the rights. Religious discrimination. We'll win."

"Be prepared to spend tens of thousands of dollars."

"We don't have tens of thousands of dollars," I said.

"And you won't win. Even if you had a good case, which you don't, good luck getting an attorney to take it. The University of California, San Diego has a ton of influence in this area. They employ a lot of people. You won't find a jury that would vote against them. I doubt you could find a judge that'd let it get to a jury. The courts protect large businesses and universities that are important to the community."

So we dropped it. Maybe at some point, a few years from now, when we're long gone from the university, Mark can write another paper. At another school. Putting a different spin on it.

"I guarantee you, I'll read my employment contract next time," Mark had said. "If that clause is in it, I'm going to demand they take it out."

The attorney doubted it was in most contracts. He'd never seen it before. Of course, Mark had signed it without reading it. The contract was ten pages long and filled with legalese. Didn't really matter. He wouldn't have gotten the job had he made it an issue at the time. Apparently, it's non-negotiable.

The university was beyond paranoid about controlling the dissemination of information. It may have been burned in the past. Regardless, we had no choice but to accept the fact that there was nothing we could do about it.

The article was on hold for now. Maybe forever.

"Life is what we make of it," I said. "This is an opportunity for a new beginning. I'm excited about it."

It felt good to speak the words, even if they weren't true. I was terrified of what was going to happen next. I didn't want to move. It seemed like we might not have a choice.

"I shouldn't have quit," he blurted, after slumping deep into the couch in despair.

It almost moved me to tears to see him in this much pain. That's also the first time I'd heard him say those words. Up until now, he'd always been defiant.

Mark was clearly going through the stages of grief. The first few weeks were anger. Now, he was somewhere between depression and acceptance. Once classes were over and he cleared out his office, I expected it to hit him hard. At some point, he'd snap out of it. I just didn't know when.

I was prepared to be there for him every step of the way. To help him through the process. Starting tonight.

It took some effort, because I had my own thoughts and emotions. I didn't think he should've quit either. Didn't think so at the time and don't think so now. It had been an impulsive act. Totally out of character for him.

Mark wasn't impulsive. He should've accepted the board's decision and regrouped. I understand why he didn't. He was hurt. And offended. The article was like a child he had birthed. He felt rejected. He had been so excited about the article. While he knew rejection was a possibility, I don't think he believed it would happen.

"It's water under the bridge," I said, putting a little enthusiasm behind my words. "I think we should trust God. He has better things in store for us in the future."

He sat there with a sad puppy dog look. I moved in closer and made him look me in the eyes by clasping both sides of his face with my hands.

"Even though you can't publish your theory, it's still an accomplishment. I'm proud of you. And we have each other. That's the most important thing. We get to grow old together. We'll have our ups and downs. This is one of the down times. We'll get through it. I promise."

The words were bolstering my spirit. I had wanted Mark to swallow his pride and ask for his job back, but he wouldn't do it. Now, sitting there on the couch, I decided that I agreed with the decision. If the university was that anti-God, then Mark would have more problems down the line. Maybe we were dodging a bullet.

Who knows what the future holds?

We had no idea how God could use this for our good, but we had the assurances in the Bible that he would.

And the whole debacle had been good for Mark. He'd become somewhat of a religious fanatic over the last two years and especially over the last eight weeks. He was on fire for Jesus.

He'd already been reprimanded twice by the dean for speaking about God in the classroom. It'd be better to be in an environment where he could teach more freely.

At the moment, we had no idea where that might be.

We talked about moving to the Midwest or going back to Santa Cruz. They'd hire him back in a second. The problem was that almost all universities had taken a turn for the worse. Not only in California, but around the country. Progressive policies had overrun most colleges and the institutions were openly hostile to conservative values and the things of God.

A private Christian college seemed like the best option but the ones that had an astronomy department were few and far between. Mark's pay would be cut in half. At least.

He hadn't started looking for a job yet. His employment contract also prevented him from seeking another position while he held this one. Another way the university controlled him. All their employees for that matter.

The attorney said that clause was set in stone as well. If Mark left early, he'd be in breach of contract, and they could sue him. If he started looking for a job until he was out of his contract, he'd also be in breach. They might not sue him, but they could make it difficult for him to get another job if they wanted.

The timing was problematic. That clause made it nearly impossible for professors and staff to leave. Which might be the purpose behind it. Most colleges and universities already had their staff in place for the fall semester.

Mark had an impressive enough resume to possibly overcome that problem, but he had no guarantees Dr. Steele would give him a good reference even if he did obey the letter of the contract. Perhaps the opposite. She might actually sabotage his attempts to get another job.

That remained to be seen.

Maybe all this was hitting Mark at once. I'd been thinking about it since the moment I learned he quit. My emotions had been on a roller coaster. Trying to put on a good face, but also worried about our future.

Mostly worried about my husband. I was confident he would bounce back from it, but I had no idea the toll this might take on him. His confidence was shattered.

At least talking about his class tomorrow and drawing the names out of the hat, had caused him to perk up somewhat. He loved the heart of Pluto presentations. It was his favorite day of the year.

I wished I felt the same about tomorrow. I was having lunch with my girlfriends.

Mark's eyes suddenly widened. He bolted off the couch.

"Come with me."

"Where?"

"Out on the deck."

"Why?" I asked.

"I almost forgot. Tonight's the blue moon."

He took my hand and pulled me off the couch and led me outside. The moon wasn't hard to spot. A full moon illuminated the sky. There wasn't a cloud anywhere.

I was confused.

"How come it's not blue?" I asked.

Mark chuckled. "It doesn't have anything to do with color."

"Then why is it called a blue moon?"

"Well . . ."

I was about to find out. A long drawn-out explanation was forthcoming. I wrapped my arm through Mark's and we leaned together against the deck railing and stared at the moon that was low on the horizon.

"It takes 354 days to complete 12 lunar cycles," Mark explained.

"Okay."

Not sure what that had to do with the color blue.

"The moon phases take 29.5 days to complete. Every two and a half years a thirteenth full moon is observed from earth."

"Is that where we get the term 'once in a blue moon'? Because it's so rare?"

"Exactly. Although, to an astronomer, two and a half years is not rare. It's fairly frequent in astronomical terms."

"The last two and a half years have certainly flown by for me."

Mark straightened and put his arm around me. I leaned against his shoulder. He stared up at the moon and let out an approving moan. I relished his warmth even though it was a nice evening and I wasn't cold at all.

"February will never experience a blue moon since it only has twenty-eight days," Mark continued. "Twenty-nine days in leap years."

"That makes sense."

He pulled me closer.

"Sometimes, February doesn't have a full moon at all. That's known as a Black Moon. Again, having nothing to do with color."

"These must've been named by men," I quipped. "Women would've never named them after colors for no reason."

"You're probably right. Although, blood moons are red."

"That's like a man. Get one out of three names correct. Too bad Eve wasn't created when Adam named the animals. He could've used her help. Aardvark. I think Eve could've come up with something better."

He grunted an agreement.

Neither of us said anything for what seemed like several minutes. We simply took in the moment and shared the intimacy. Mark was fixated on the moon. I was fixated on him.

An idea came to me.

"Have you ever made love under a blue moon?" I asked, in a seductive voice.

"I can't say that I have."

"Wait right here."

I went inside and found a blanket.

Mark's blue eyes were as bright as the moon in the sky, when he saw me lay the blanket down on the back deck and begin taking off my clothes.

This'll make him feel better.

***

The next morning

The country club was bustling. A line of golfers waited on the first tee to start their rounds. It looked like some kind of local tournament. The restaurant was packed, but my ladies were well connected, and we were seated immediately at the best table.

For whatever reason, the ladies picked me to start sharing intimate details.

"When are you and Mark going to have a baby?" Page asked, out of the blue and before we had even ordered our drinks.

I hesitated. "Well, Mark and I have been trying for several years now."

"We know that, silly," Page said. "You told us that several years ago. Driving over here, it dawned on me that you still don't have one. What are you waiting for?"

I didn't remember mentioning it, but she might be right.

"God. And it never seems like the right time."

"Your biological clock is ticking," Page said, sending a jolt of anger through me.

"You sound like my mother."

"All Bill had to do was look at me and I got pregnant," Trista said. "After Bill Jr. I got fixed. I didn't want any more kids. Especially with him."

Bill and Trista were the only couple other than us who were still married. The other three ladies were divorced and had new boyfriends. At least they did the last time we got together. They might have different boyfriends today.

The last time we met was before Mark quit his job. A fact they probably didn't know. We hadn't told anyone other than my parents, our pastor, and the members of our lifegroup.

"At first, we were waiting for Mark to get out of school," I said. "You know. We couldn't really afford another mouth to feed."

London waved her hand dismissively.

"That's what you think at the time, but you would've managed."

"I know. But school was demanding, and Mark was never home. I was working at the time to support us. My parents couldn't help. Our insurance wasn't great. It didn't seem like a good time."

"It's tough starting out," Rhea said. "I wished we had waited. I mean, don't get me wrong, I love Laney, but I never thought I'd have to raise her alone."

She wasn't really raising her teenage daughter alone. Her ex-husband had Laney more than half the time. And he had his girlfriend to help. But I knew what she meant and wasn't about to correct her.

I was just glad the topic was off of me.

Or so I thought.

"You said that you've been trying for a while," Trista said. "Are you not able to get pregnant?"

"Not so far," I said.

"How long have you been trying?"

"Three years."

"Wow! That's a long time."

"I know."

"Have you seen a doctor?"

"That's our next step."

"I know a guy. He's a friend of a friend. Actually, he shares a building with my plastic surgeon."

Trista had probably paid for that building with all the work she had done.

"I don't think we can afford it," I said, sheepishly. "I think it's like twenty thousand dollars or more per time."

"Mark is a professor," Trista said. "I'm sure he makes good money now."

"Actually ... I have news. Mark is no longer at the school. Today is his last day."

"Oh my word! What happened? I thought he had tenure."

"He does have tenure. He quit."

"Quit!"

"Why?"

"What happened?"

"It's a long story."

"We've got all day."

The ladies loved gossip. They were sitting forward in their seats. I wasn't usually the source of such drama.

The waiter arrived about that time to take our drink order. Thankfully. It gave me time to gather my thoughts and decide how much I was willing to tell them. Everyone ordered cocktails. I ordered my standard iced tea.

I wasn't sure which was more uncomfortable. Talking about my fertility or Mark losing his job. Mark had a non-disclosure agreement in his employment contract. He couldn't reveal the details of his employment to any third party. Which extended to me, so I manipulated the conversation toward my fertility. Or lack thereof.

"We don't know why I can't get pregnant," I said.

"We've never been tested to see who has the problem."

"We're just trusting God."

I left out most of the details. Including how frustrating it had been for us. I cried almost every month when my cycle started.

Talking about babies was too painful and so I changed the subject to Mark's job.

"Mark wrote an article for a science journal," I said. "I told you about it. He worked on it for over two years. The university decided not to publish it, so Mark quit. No hard feelings or anything. He felt like he needed a change of scenery. Maybe teach at a school more open to his ideas."

"I had no idea," Page said, sincerely. In a rare moment of empathy for her. "Does this mean you're going to move away from here?"

"Probably."

The ladies let out a collective groan. "No! Where would you move to?"

"We are thinking about the Midwest. That's where Mark is from. Maybe a private college somewhere."

"I thought Mark was happy here."

"He was. I mean, he is, we are. But there aren't a lot of opportunities here for him."

It was hitting me all at once. It really would be a huge adjustment. I'd gotten used to being back home. I'd miss my parents. Our church. The weather. Even my girlfriends.

"There aren't many work options in California," I said, almost angrily. "Most of the universities are liberal bastions. The private colleges might be more open to God and Mark's views on science and would certainly love to have someone of his stature."

"I thought UCSD was the best of the best," London said.

"It is. Mark is really disappointed. We both are."

It seemed so unfair.

"Maybe he can take a job in private industry," Trista said. She owned a successful business and was the richest and most successful by far, even though all the other ladies were millionaires several times over.

"He'd probably make three times what he makes at the university," she added.

"I don't know. Mark loves to teach. He'd be miserable clocking in at an 8 to 5 job."

"We don't want you to move," Trista whined.

"We don't want to move either. We might not have a choice."

An alarm went off on my phone interrupting the conversation. Surprisingly, since I had it on silent. The alarm was so loud, it echoed through the restaurant and several people turned and looked our way.

I reached for my purse.

At the same time, a commotion occurred inside the restaurant. A number of patrons rushed toward a television set by the bar.

I couldn't see what all the fuss was about from our vantage point.

I found my phone and switched off the annoying alarm and touched the main screen which had a notification on it.

From the university.

What?

An alert.

I opened it. My mouth flew open, and my heart started racing when I read the words.

LOCKDOWN! LIGHTS! OUT OF SIGHT!

ACTIVE SHOOTER! ACTIVE THREAT!

EMERGENCY PROTOCOLS IN PLACE!

I'd seen these before. The university often ran tests. I received the alerts because I was a spouse of an employee. It went out to all the students, faculty, and staff. Anyone associated with the university.

My first thought was that this was a test.

THIS IS NOT A TEST!

My heart began to race.

"What's going on?" Trista asked. "You look like you've seen a ghost."

"What's all the commotion about over there?" London asked. Pointing at the television set.

"There's an active shooter at Mark's school," I said. My whole body was shaking.

I stood to my feet. "I've got to go."

Trista was sitting next to me and grabbed my arm.

"Where are you going?"

"To the school? To find Mark. He's teaching a class."

"The school is on lockdown."

"I know."

"You can't go to the school. There's an active shooter. I'm sure Mark is fine. He got the alert as well and is taking precautions."

"I'm going to call him."

The call went to voicemail.

I started crying. Uncontrollably.

8

Last day of class

By the time class started, Mark was over his doldrums. The time to mourn the loss of his teaching position was after the class was over. Not before and certainly not during. He wasn't about to let Dr. Steele or the powers that be rob him of the joy of his last Heart of Pluto class at the University of California, San Diego.

Selena Sanchez was up first. One of the rare Hispanics to take his class over the years. Even with the large Hispanic population in Southern California, only one percent of Hispanics studied astronomy. Ninety percent were white. Only one percent black. Asians made up about 6.7 percent and the rest were other nationalities.

Selena went first because she had graphics. Her computer was already hooked up to the audio-visual system and the best picture in Mark's opinion of the heart of Pluto was on vivid display for the class to see.

"Not only does Pluto have a heart," Selena began, "it has a heartbeat. At this time, I'm going to show you two different pictures."

Two close-up pictures of the ice that formed the heart were side by side on the screen. Selena had a pointer in her hand, which was noticeably shaking. As was her voice.

"The two pictures were taken hours apart," she explained. "Of the same region of the heart. Notice how the ice in the picture on the left is different from the picture on the right. Its peaks are higher."

"Are you going to explain why they are different?" Mark asked.

"Of course."

This should be interesting.

"The ice is made up of frozen nitrogen," she said.

Not breaking news. Most scientists agreed with that hypothesis.

"The nitrogen is frozen on the surface which is a balmy 450 degrees below zero."

The class let out an obligatory chuckle. That seemed to relax her some as Mark saw her shoulders loosen a bit.

"During the day, the frozen nitrogen melts and vaporizes. The vapor hovers over the surface. Some escapes into the atmosphere. Some creates the winds of Pluto."

"Do you know what the speed of the winds are?" Mark asked.

"Twenty-three miles per hour. Roughly. Although, scientists once thought the wind speeds were much higher."

"Here's a little known fact," Mark said. "The air on Pluto is so thin, if the winds were hundreds of miles per hour, you'd still barely feel them."

"Ahh. Interesting."

"You may continue, Selena."

Mark liked to interrupt them. To see if they had done more than just copy what was on the internet. To see if they had actually conducted research. Curveball questions gave him an idea as to the depth of their knowledge. He was pleased that Selena knew the wind speed. Although, scientists didn't really know for sure. The probe hadn't conducted any experiments.

"At night, the frozen nitrogen that is left over, re-freezes on the surface. So the height of the basin varies depending on the time of day. It's like the heart is breathing. More specifically, it's beating like a heart. Expanding in and out."

The students asked a few questions which Mark always allowed them to do. He didn't even care if the class went long that day. Whenever it ended would be too soon. If he were honest, he didn't want it to end. He'd desperately miss teaching at this prestigious school. Regardless of his feelings of distrust for those who ran it.

"Do you have a theory as to what caused the crater?" Mark asked.

"I like your theory," she said. "That it was caused by a nuclear war."

"Agreeing with me will get you an automatic A," Mark said, to a generous laugh from the other students.

"I agree with you!"

"Me too!"

"All right. That's enough brown nosing of the teacher."

They didn't know they were all getting A's anyway.

Selena finished her presentation. She waited to see if Mark had any more questions. He didn't.

"Thank you, Selena. For a well thought out presentation. I've never really heard anyone call it a heartbeat before. That's interesting."

The class applauded enthusiastically as she took her seat. Caesar Howe made his way to the front without being asked. Mark decided to let the students know at the beginning of the class who'd be making a presentation. Normally, he surprised them. This time he wanted to give them time to prepare. Time to get nervous.

The other students couldn't relax though. The last name was a secret. That way everyone had to be ready in case their name was called. Even though Mark knew who'd be last. He'd set the order on purpose.

"Ladies and gentlemen, this is Mr. Caesar Howe."

The class applauded again.

"Let's hear your theory."

"I believe that a moon crashed into Pluto causing the crater."

That spurred a fifteen-minute discussion. Caesar admitted he had nothing to back up the theory other than speculation. Of course, Mark had no proof an atomic war on the surface between two warring factions was the cause either. It was a plausible theory even though the crater clearly wasn't moon shaped.

"Zoe is next," Mark said.

Mark had been looking forward to her presentation. She'd given him a hint a couple of weeks before as to the direction of her paper when she came to him in private and asked some specific questions about the tilt of Pluto. Which was drastically different from earth's tilt.

She began by explaining the difference. The tilt was fascinating. Another strange phenomenon on Pluto. Pluto was such an enigma. Which was what made it so fascinating to Mark.

"The earth tilts at 23.5 degrees," Zoe said. "Pluto's tilt is nearly 120 degrees. It rotates around the sun practically on its side."

"What do you think causes the tilt?" Mark asked.

"I was getting to that, Professor."

"Please proceed."

"The ice in the crater is heavy and weighs down the planet, causing it to lean. Exaggerating the tilt. The crater is caused by the outer surface cracking because of the weight."

"What keeps the planet from tilting over completely, and tumbling out of its orbit?" Mark asked.

"Some day it might. As the ice continues to build up, it might someday cause it to tip over from the top. In a few more years, we can measure how fast the ice is increasing, then we can make that calculation."

"That'd certainly be fun to watch," one of the students said.

Everyone laughed, including Mark.

Mark would've liked to spend more time on the tilt discussion, but he was running out of time. So he called the next student. Alaric Rogers.

"The heart was caused by aliens."

Mark had told his standard joke about giving an F to whoever floated that theory. Almost every class, someone reciprocated in their presentation. Mark pretended to be writing down a bad grade.

The presentation wasn't that good. Alaric would get a C under normal circumstances. He only regurgitated what could be googled rather easily.

Mark had already decided everyone would get an A in the class, regardless. As long as they came to class and made an effort. His last gift to the students and a parting shot to the administration.

It'd also make recording the grades easier. His employment contract continued until he posted the final grades. Then his tenure with the university was over. He wanted to get it over with as soon as possible and move on to the next chapter of his life. As soon as the class was over, he'd go back to his office, post the grades, then clear out his desk.

The administration had robbed him from the opportunity to say goodbye since no one but Mia knew his employment was ending. Once it did, he still had a non-disclosure agreement to abide by. Next fall, the students would show up and his wouldn't be on the list of available classes. No explanation would be offered.

The final student was Vanessa Hodges. He chose her because she was a Christian. Vanessa was a friend of Lee Barrett. She knew about the article. Not from Mark. He could never reveal anything to anyone about what had happened.

Lee was under no such restrictions, and he openly discussed his displeasure with what he considered to be religious discrimination.

What could the school do to him? Nothing. They could suspend him, but that'd only bolster his argument.

"I'll sue," Lee had said.

Mark didn't necessarily try to dissuade him. Lee and the other students had put a lot of work into the article. The peer review's decision was clearly discriminatory. Not based on merit but religious bias.

Something the Constitution was supposed to protect Christians from. All religions for that matter. Would they have rejected the article had Mark written that Buddha or Allah formed the heart?

He wondered. They'd never know, but the diversity preaching woke administration preached tolerance for everyone but those of the Christian faith.

Lee had formed a Bible study at the school that met in the afternoons once a week on campus. The school refused to give him permission and wouldn't sanction it as a social club, so they met in private.

Vanessa attended the Bible study. They asked Mark to speak, and he accepted, but didn't bring up anything about Pluto or the article.

He halfway expected Vanessa to mention his theory in her presentation. He wasn't going to stop her. What could they do to him? It's not like he was getting a severance package that they could hold over his head. A reference would be helpful, but he didn't really need it. Santa Cruz would provide a great reference. He could even go back there if he wanted.

No one knew today was his last day. Including Lee. Since this was the last presentation, a sadness began to come over him.

Vanessa was bubbly and outgoing and helped him get over it. She was full of spunk and personality. The other students liked her in spite of her constant attempts to evangelize them.

"Over the last two years, Dr. Cooper, along with several students, wrote an article promoting a theory as to the heart of Pluto."

Mark grimaced on the inside. But he kept quiet. What could Dr. Steele do? He didn't tell her and he wasn't the one who told the class that fact.

"The basic premise was that God formed the heart as a sign," she continued.

You could hear a pin drop in the room between sentences.

"The main theory in the article was that a nuclear war on Pluto caused the heart shape."

"What caused the nuclear war?" one of the students asked.

"One of Dr. Cooper's assumptions in the article was that Pluto had intelligent life on it. Like Earth."

Several of the students looked in Mark's direction. He kept his eyes fixed on Vanessa.

"How did they survive in 450 below zero temperature?" one of the students asked.

Mark intended to keep his mouth shut.

"With God, all things are possible," Vanessa answered confidently.

He was proud of her for standing up for her faith.

Someone noticeably scoffed. Mark wasn't sure who.

"Anyway, I think that Dr. Cooper is wrong," she said.

The class murmured. Then looked at Mark to make sure he wasn't offended. He flashed a broad smile, letting him know he wasn't.

They began to razz him. To razz her.

She quieted them down without Mark having to. She had a commanding presence in that way.

"Tell me where I'm wrong," Mark said. "I always encourage open and frank discussion in my classroom. If I'm wrong, I will admit it."

"I don't believe the crater was caused by a nuclear war between different factions on Pluto."

"If it wasn't a nuclear war, then what do you think caused it?" Mark asked.

"I didn't say it wasn't a nuclear war."

"I think that's what you said," one of the students said.

"No. What I said was that it wasn't a nuclear war on Pluto. I believe it was a nuclear war between Pluto and Neptune."

Mark's mouth flew open.

"Why do you think that?" he asked.

"We've had a number of nuclear explosions on earth. In Japan and in numerous islands where the US conducted tests. Other countries have exploded bombs as well. They don't leave a crater the size of the heart on Pluto."

"How big is the crater?"

"Almost six hundred miles of area. It'd take millions of nuclear bombs to create a crater that size."

She waited for Mark to respond. When he didn't, she continued.

"To make a crater that big and that deep would require momentum. Lee and I did the calculations. It's in my paper. What we found is that one nuclear bomb from Neptune could hit Pluto with enough velocity and momentum to create a crater of that size."

Interesting.

"I think the two planets were warring. One of them, Neptune, had a nuclear bomb and destroyed all life on Pluto, killing everyone and sending a huge debris field into the Kuiser Belt."

If only they could test it. A probe could take samples from the waste material in the belt and determine if nuclear material was present. It might even find the DNA of humans on it.

Somehow, Mark needed to get this article published. This might be the angle he needed to publish it at another school. This was not the same theory he had proposed in the article written while a member of the faculty here at UCSD.

He was suddenly excited to leave. To begin working on this theory. He'd invite Lee and Vanessa to his house, and they could help him research it. As long as it wasn't on campus, there was nothing Dr. Steele could do about it.

Vanessa finished her presentation, but Mark hardly heard anything she said. His mind was elsewhere. His heart was leaping with enthusiasm at the possibilities of a new discovery. He couldn't wait to look at their formula and see if it was correct.

He walked to the front of the class.

"Thank you, everyone for your presentations. I thoroughly enjoyed them. And I loved having all of you as my students. It's been my pleasure."

They applauded.

He wasn't ready to dismiss them. This became a teaching moment. The last one for this class. The last one for any students of University of California, San Diego.

"Vanessa has got me thinking. Maybe I am wrong. Let this be a lesson to all of you. Don't become so connected to your theories that you aren't open to other ideas."

He took in a deep breath. Not sure if he could say the thought that had popped into his head. He decided to say it anyway.

"Only two things are infinite. God and human stupidity."

Everyone laughed.

"As humans, we don't have all the answers to the mysteries of the universe. I'm glad we don't. It makes us hungry for knowledge. Don't ever lose your desire to learn. Until the day I die, I hope to be learning something new. Everyday."

"Is anything in science finite?" Caesar asked. "Are we supposed to assume that no truth exists?"

"It's not that everything is theoretically possible. Because it's not. The truth exists. That's what we are searching for. The opposite is true. Everything is theoretically impossible in my mind, until I can prove it."

He paused for effect.

"Aerodynamically, it's impossible for a bumble bee to fly. And yet it does. Because it doesn't know better. No one has told a bee that it can't fly, so it does. That's how you should approach science. Don't let anyone tell you that you can't think for yourself. That you have to limit your ideas to what they think."

He started to tell them to be open to the possibility of God but decided against it. This wasn't a sermon.

"Research is like going on a blind date," Mark said. "You don't know what you're going to find until you take a step of faith and go on the date. You may reject him or her. Or you may find the most beautiful thing in the whole world and your life will change."

Mark thought of Mia and his heart warmed. He loved her so much. Was so thankful for her.

"Science, my friends, is full of mistakes," Mark said. "If you make enough mistakes along the way, you may stumble upon the truth. If you kiss enough frogs, you may find a prince."

They all laughed. Mark moved from behind his desk to the front and leaned back against it.

"So, keep going on blind dates," he said. "Eventually, you may find the love of your life. Whatever you do in your life, keep trying new things. Keep searching for the truth. Someday, you may stumble upon it and your life will never be the same."

They applauded when it became apparent that he was finished.

"It's been a pleasure teaching you this semester."

They stood to their feet and gave him a standing ovation.

Mark smiled warmly.

"Pass your papers to the front. And you're dismissed. I hope you have a great summer."

As he spoke the last words, Mark heard a sound coming from the hallway. It sounded like firecrackers.

More like a car backfiring.

That wasn't possible since the building was several hundred yards from the street. You had to walk a distance from the parking lot to get to the building.

The next sounds were horrifying. Unmistakably gunshots and screams. Coming from the other end of the hall.

A panic shot through Mark. A class was meeting on that end of the floor.

Was there a gunman in the building?

"Everyone get away from the door!" Mark said.

He walked over to the window on the door and peeked out. He couldn't see anything, so he cracked it open and stuck his head out.

What he saw was horrifying.

Down at the other end of the hall was a man holding a rifle. Another rifle was draped over his back. He had a belt with a handgun strapped to his waist and what looked like ammunition in the belt.

The man was cloaked in body armor. The body of a student lay on the floor in a pool of blood.

Mark closed the door.

"There's a gunman outside this door," Mark said, barely above a whisper. "I'm going to slip out into the hall. I want you all to barricade this door and don't let anyone but me or the authorities in."

The students seemed to be in a state of shock.

"I'll go with you," Caesar said.

"You stay here. Help put the desks against the door. Don't let anyone in. Call 911."

Mark didn't wait for an objection. He opened the door and shut it quietly behind him.

The gunman was at the other end of the hall with his back to him. Mark began moving quietly toward him.

He's headed for the other classroom!

Were they still in there? Maybe. If they were, he could kill everyone in the class.

Someone had to stop him. Mark was the only person in the hallway.

Without giving it another thought, Mark took off sprinting. Toward the man. The man must've seen him from the corner of his eye or heard the sounds of his footsteps, because he turned.

Mark was close. He opened fire. The automatic rifle riddled Mark with bullets.

It felt like someone had stabbed him with a thousand hot pokers.

He ignored the pain and lowered his shoulder. His momentum carried him into the man and knocked them both to the ground.

A cracking sound.

The man's head smacked against the concrete floor.

Mark landed on top of him.

The man was stunned. Mark had the presence of mind to use his weight to hold him down.

The man was dazed.

He moved slightly. Mark was losing strength. Blood was pouring from his stomach and chest.

Mark grabbed the gunman's hair and slammed his head into the floor again. Knocking him unconscious.

He rolled off of him onto the floor.

That's when everything went black.

Then bright lights.

Within seconds, maybe minutes, maybe instantly, Mark knew exactly what had happened on Pluto.

9

The funeral for Dr. Mark Cooper and the three students who lost their lives two and a half weeks ago was moved from the UCSD fine arts auditorium to the LionTree Arena. It held 4000 people for basketball, but more than 4500 people were packed in and several thousand more watched from outside on the monitors set up around campus.

Untold millions watched on television as all the local stations and every major cable news channel carried it live. The governor of California attended along with the vice president of the United States. The president delivered remarks shortly after the shooting using the opportunity to promote his gun control initiative and did not attend although he sent the first lady.

Both senators from California and several members of Congress were there as well. I thought it might be more for the publicity than anything else, but I tried not to be too cynical.

The nationwide outpouring was heartwarming.

I wanted to have Mark's funeral at our church, but eventually relented when the powers that be at the university were insistent. Even if I doubted the sincerity of some involved, it made sense to have the funerals together. I couldn't deny that the school shooting had affected everyone in the community in a profound way.

Whatever resentment I held for Dr. Steele and the events leading up to Mark's last day at school, didn't overshadow the fact that the school shooting was bigger than me. I couldn't be petty at a time like this.

Dr. Steele called me into her office to discuss it.

"Mark is a hero," she had said. "He saved countless lives."

That was true. Hadden Cohen, twenty-four-years-old, entered the science building armed with an AR-15 military style rifle, and a 9 mm handgun with enough ammunition to shoot up a small army. The former student suffered from an emotional disorder, and snapped when his girlfriend broke up with him the week before.

She was a student in another class in the building. The gunman was standing directly outside the classroom about to enter. Cohen posted several rants on social media that morning, claiming he intended to kill his girlfriend along with everyone in the building. Two classes were meeting that day. One with 22 students, Mark's class, and 30 in the ex-girlfriend's class. Two students were killed outside the building. Wrong place at the wrong time. They happened to be passing by the building at the moment the shooter was preparing to enter.

After killing them, Cohen entered the building and chained the door from the inside. He shot and killed a student in the hall returning to class from a restroom break.

That's when Mark acted.

The entire incident was caught on security cameras in the hallway. The loop had been played hundreds of times on the news and millions of times online, but I'd never seen it. And never intended to.

"This tragedy could've been a lot worse if not for him," Dr. Steele added.

"That's the Mark I knew," I said to her. "He loved his students."

"Yes, he did. He was a great teacher."

The whole conversation was awkward. For her and for me.

"He loved working here," I said, daring to mention the elephant in the room hovering over both of us. "He was going to miss it."

I saw her grimace slightly. To my knowledge, the circle of people who knew that Mark was leaving the university was small. So far, the press hadn't gotten word of it. I doubted the university would say anything and I certainly wasn't going to.

Dr. Steele leaned forward in her chair. I sat in one of the two chairs across from her desk.

"I wanted to let you know that the university has an insurance policy that covers our faculty and staff in the event of a school shooting."

I didn't say anything. That had been something I hadn't allowed myself to think about. Mark didn't have a life insurance policy. I received what I thought was his last paycheck the day before. My attorney had mentioned possibly suing the university, but I'd put that off for a later date. I had to bury my husband first.

Eventually, I'd have to move from our house if I didn't get some money. I was already thinking about getting a job. We had six months in a savings account. One month had been used to pay for the funeral arrangements.

"Mark resigned," I blurted. "Is he still entitled to the insurance money?"

"Technically, he was still a member of the faculty."

"I thought his tenure ended on the last day of school."

"His class wasn't over. He was still covered by our policy. Ironically, for another twenty minutes or so."

"Okay. What does that mean?"

"The payout is three million dollars. You should receive it within ten days."

I about fell out of the chair.

"Thank you. I don't know what to say."

"I want to remind you that Mark's employment agreement has a non-disclosure clause. You signed it as well when he started at the university."

"I know. I don't intend to say anything."

"Good. We don't either. As far as we're concerned, Mark was a professor in good standing at our university. Which is true. I see no reason to diminish that fact by confusing people with something that's not important now anyway. That's why he needs to be a part of the memorial service."

"I want my pastor to speak at the service," I said.

"Of course."

"He'll mention God."

"That's fine. I'll mention God myself. We all should consider God at a time like this."

And Dr. Steele did mention God. Even quoted the Bible.

"There is a river whose streams make glad the city of God," she said, quoting Psalms 46.

"God is within her. She shall not fail."

I tried my best to hold it together. I sat on the stage which was set up at one end of the floor level. The seats surrounded us. The stage was packed with people. The immediate family members of the three students sat on one side with the president of the university and the chancellor.

I sat on the other side with Dr. Steele, the other faculty members in the science department, and my pastor. The dignitaries sat in the middle behind the podium.

Before the service started, I had an emotional gathering in the back room with the family members of the other victims. We had never met and it was an emotional time as they kept thanking me profusely.

They weren't on stage, but I also met the parents of the shooter's girlfriend. Their daughter wasn't there for obvious reasons. They told me she was torn up about it. Blaming herself. I tried to reassure them that it wasn't her fault.

"Mark was a man of deep faith," Dr. Steele said, startling me. "I admire that about him."

I bet you did.

I scolded myself. Now wasn't the time to let bitterness take root. The whole incident with Mark's Pluto paper was still eating away at my insides. So unfair that Mark's last days were filled with such turmoil. Through no fault of his own.

I'd already been thinking about how I might find a way to publish Mark's paper. Take advantage of his fifteen minutes of fame to put it out there. I was within ten feet of a couple of senators. I considered talking to them about funding another mission to Pluto. Now might be the best time to approach them.

My attorney said not to mention the paper to anyone.

"I told my pastor."

"Don't tell anyone else."

"What are they going to do?" I said. "Sue me? The grieving widow?"

"That's exactly what they'd do. And get an injunction to prevent you from doing so."

"What if I simply put it out on the internet? Didn't publish it. Just posted it online. What could they do about it?"

"As your attorney, I'm advising you not to do it."

I still didn't know what I was going to do.

What I needed to do was focus. A million cameras were on me. At least it seemed like it. Trying to get a shot of the heartbroken widow from every angle. I didn't want to have them speculating on why I had a scowl on my face while Dr. Steele was talking.

"Our university was shattered by the gunman's bullets," Dr. Steele said. "I've walked that very hallway thousands of times. Never in my wildest dreams could I have imagined that our science building could become ground zero for such a senseless tragedy."

I couldn't either. It all still seemed like a dream.

When I kissed Mark that morning and he went off to class, I had no idea that'd be the last time I saw him. My heart ached just thinking about it. That I'd never kiss him again. Never send him off to work again. Never feel his touch again.

Tears welled up in my eyes. I'd been holding them back. The emotional dam wasn't that strong. I dabbed at my eyes with a tissue. It'd take every bit of self-control to keep from sobbing.

I wore a white dress.

I know. I'm supposed to wear black.

Mark would've been angry with me had I worn black. The few times we talked about our mortality he was adamant that I wasn't to shed any tears for him. That he was in heaven with Jesus.

"Don't wear black to my funeral," he had said. "That's too morbid. Make it a celebration."

Our pastor would mention it, so the media outlets wouldn't rake me over the coals for my lack of decorum. I could hear the pundits critiquing my outfit.

"Dr. Mark Cooper was a remarkable man."

Thankfully, Dr. Steele's remarks were about over.

"Our university will be stronger for having known him. The courage and will of Dr. Mark Cooper is alive in the spirit of all of us. He will be missed."

I wonder if he would've been missed had the shooting never happened.

No way. At the time, they were glad he was leaving.

Dr. Steele wasn't quite finished.

"I have an announcement to make. Dr. Mark Cooper has left an indelible mark, pun intended, on this university. He is a remarkable and distinct visionary. Because of that, we are renaming the science building after Mark. Starting today, it will be known as Cooper Hall."

The applause forced a smile on my face. I already knew that fact. Dr. Steele asked me for permission the day before. At first, I started to object. Then thought it foolish. At least some good could come of this. Mark deserved to be honored and remembered.

And I had to dutifully play the part and keep the dark thoughts out of my head. What I really wanted to do was yawn. I hadn't gotten much sleep, and the speakers were boring me. My body ached from trying to dutifully sit in the proper position for the cameras.

The governor spoke too long. I don't think he even mentioned Mark. Maybe he did. It sounded more like a campaign speech.

The vice president's speech started out strong and was inspiring. Of course, he had good speech writers who would know just what to say.

"To the families of the victims, to the students of this fine university, to the people of California, and to the millions of fellow Americans who are watching, we are united in grief."

He turned and looked at me and then over at the families.

"There's nothing I can say or do that will fill the sudden hole in your lives. I will not even attempt to do so."

I wanted to burst into tears, but somehow managed to hold them back. The hole was as real as it had ever been. I didn't know how I was going to live without him. He was the love of my life.

The vice president mentioned the three students by name. Talked about each one of them individually. Mentioned their backgrounds and interests, which was a nice touch.

"Millie was an A student who should've been graduating. She loved gymnastics and was a dancer. Peter was on the water polo team. Janie was engaged to be married. Sometime next summer. After she graduated."

He got to Mark. That's when I thought I was going to lose it.

The four caskets lined the front of the stage. All of their pictures were on easels. I had avoided looking at them. Fortunately, they were turned away from me. Facing the crowd. No way to keep from seeing the caskets unless I completely turned my head away from the podium.

"Dr. Mark Cooper was one of the finest minds in America. His colleagues describe him as the most popular teacher on campus. He had a waiting list of students who wanted to be in his class."

He asked a show of hands from those who had taken one of his classes. Hands went up all over the arena.

"I'm told that he was the foremost expert in the world on the planet Pluto."

Everyone laughed.

"Actually, my mistake. I know. Before one of these distinguished professors stands up and corrects me, Pluto is not a planet. I understand that Professor Cooper believed it still should be considered a planet. That he was against declassifying it."

I nodded my head. More laughter from the crowd.

He continued. "Teaching was Dr. Cooper's passion. In reality, his true passion was helping his students. From what I've learned about him over the last few hours of spending time with his colleagues, what Mark did was not surprising to them or to me. He tackled the gunman. He didn't have any special training. He wasn't armed. He didn't have a black belt in karate. He just knew he had to do something. So he did. And he saved countless lives by doing so."

The crowd applauded for more than a minute.

"His courage is problematic for all of us. Let me tell you why. Mark didn't know that level of heroism was in his heart. He'd never been faced with that situation before. Today, he's asking each of us a question. Asking me a question. Another teaching moment from this scholar. What am I waiting to be called upon to do? When will my time come to be summoned to answer the call?"

He paused for effect. He was a good speaker.

"An even deeper question presses into my conscious mind. Beyond prayers and condolences, how can I honor the sacrifice of Dr. Mark Cooper beyond my shallow words? We need a national conversation."

Here we go. I had hoped he'd keep his liberal agenda out of it.

This audience would love it.

"Beyond the normal debate of the merits of gun control, I'd prefer we debate what could be done to prevent such a tragedy in the future. The President of the United States is establishing a task force to discuss that very thing. He has put me in charge of it. We are going to address the inadequacy of our mental health system. The availability of assault rifles. We have to discuss these things. Not to blame, but to heal."

Applause.

"Those who died here make me believe that we can do better. That we have let them down in some way. So that their deaths are not in vain, the forces of good must draw us together at a time like this. It's time to put partisanship aside. Mark didn't know if the student's he was saving were Republicans or Democrats. He didn't care. All he knew was that evil was present and had to be stopped. And stop it he did!"

The loudest applause came from that line. It sounded like the vice president was winding down his speech.

"May God bring peace to the families and eternal rest to the victims. May he bless the United States of America."

He got a standing ovation. I looked at the clock on the back of the wall. It had been well over an hour. I should've had my pastor go first rather than last. Some people in the back were leaving.

Our pastor was introduced and began. His hand held a Bible. That didn't keep his hands from shaking. I could tell he was nervous. This was definitely the biggest audience he'd ever spoken to.

"I'll keep my remarks short," Norris Chapman said, after introducing himself as Mark's pastor.

"The first three letters of the word funeral are f, u, and n. They spell fun."

He got a few chuckles. I could tell this crowd was leery of anyone called "pastor."

"Mark instructed his wife that his funeral was supposed to be a celebration. He told her to wear white, not black."

Everyone laughed. I imagine the cameras panned to me at that moment.

"Do you remember the violinists who kept playing while the Titanic was sinking?" he said. "That's what Mark wanted at his funeral. He wanted music. He wanted people not to grieve."

He sighed deeply.

"I am the first to admit that it's hard for me to celebrate. I feel for the families of these young people who had their whole lives ahead of them. My heart breaks for Mia, Mark's wife. I know how much he meant to her. Yet I must honor his wishes. I dishonor him, if I let us sink into a depression, even though the moment tempts us."

He paused and looked down at his notes. Told a few funny stories about Mark. Then got back to the core of his speech.

"So ... speaking of the Titanic, one of the men who lost his life that day was a man named John Harper. John was a pastor from Scotland. Only forty years old. He was on his way to America to preach at a church in Chicago. When the ship struck the iceberg and it was obvious they were all going down, Mark was on the deck helping people load onto the lifeboats. He refused to get one himself. It is recorded that he said. 'Let the non-Christians go first.'"

The whole place got awkwardly silent.

"Why would he say that? Because the Christians were safe. How were they safe?"

I knew my pastor wasn't going to sugarcoat the gospel, but I didn't know he was going to be this direct.

"Because their places in heaven were secure. Pastor Harper knew where he was going when he died. He was concerned about those who were about to die without Jesus. The ones who would go to hell if they died that night."

Did he just mention hell?

"This service today is not for Mark's benefit. He's not dead. He's more alive than he's ever been. This is for those of us who miss him. If he could speak to us today, he'd want everyone to know that he's fine. He'd be more concerned about those who are not fine. Those who don't know where they're going when they die."

You could hear a pin drop in the auditorium. I could imagine that the networks had gone to commercial.

I hoped not.

"If you're not ready to die, then you're not ready to live."

The preacher in him had come out. The excitement in his voice was exciting me. Mark would love it. Even if the majority of the people in the audience didn't.

He presented the plan of salvation and practically gave an altar call. Short of asking them to bow their heads or come to the front.

"Let me leave you with this one final thought about our dear friend, Mark Cooper," Norris said. "It's taken from a passage in the book of Revelation. Blessed are the dead who die in the Lord. For they may rest from their labors and their works follow them."

He took in a deep breath, looked around the vast auditorium in every direction. Including the back where the crowd encircled him.

"You're right Mr. Vice President," Norris said. "Mark was obsessed with Pluto. He'd devoted his work to studying it. He wrote a fascinating paper about the Heart of Pluto."

I saw Dr. Steele grimace.

I was cheering him on. My attorney didn't say my pastor couldn't say anything.

"Did you know Pluto has a heart on the side of it? Let me show you."

He pointed to the screen. A picture of Pluto came up with the heart clearly visible.

"Mark believed that God gave that heart to us as a sign of his great love for us."

He paused again for dramatic effect.

"I've read the paper that Mark wrote and I admit that I don't understand it all. It's filled with all kinds of numbers and equations that are above my head. I have a college degree, but I barely graduated. Do you know why the sun never went to college? Because it already has a million degrees."

Everyone laughed. He delivered the punch line perfectly. They might not have liked the content, but they were enjoying the delivery.

"Revelation says that their works follow them. I hope wherever Mark is today, he's got a better view of Pluto. That his work has followed him."

Applause.

His tone turned sober.

"I'll say this. That heart of Pluto is big. I read in Mark's paper that it's a thousand miles across at its widest point. I only knew Mark for three years, but I can tell you this. Pluto doesn't have a bigger heart than Mark Cooper."

He looked up to heaven and pointed.

"We'll miss you, my friend."

I thought I would burst into tears. Even though my heart was filled with joy.

I did miss Mark. But I could see my future now. My purpose.

I had to figure out how to get that paper published.

10

Three months later

For the first time since Mark's funeral, I met my girlfriends for lunch at the country club. It's amazing how much things can change in three months. The last time we met, Page and Trista were married; London and Rhea were divorced. This time, it was the other way around. Sort of.

Last time, I was . . .

I promised myself, I wasn't going to cry in front of them and was determined to fulfill the promise. We'd been there twenty minutes, and the girls were too self-absorbed to get around to talking about how I was doing. Which was fine by me.

Trista didn't follow through on her threat to vote with her brothers and sell the company that had been in her family for more than a hundred years. Instead, she went a step further and voted with her brothers to have her husband ousted as the CEO.

I choked down a gasp. The others were shocked as well.

Her husband Bill was livid. Trista felt bad about it at first and was going to change her mind about the whole thing. Until her husband moved out of their twenty thousand square foot mansion and into his girlfriend's apartment.

A girlfriend of five years Trista didn't know he had. To make matters worse, the woman worked at the company and Trista knew her fairly well. The shrew, as Trista called her, was terminated immediately although she threatened to sue for sexual harassment and might've won had she not let Bill move in with her. Hard to claim you were harassed when you invite the abuser to live with you.

The whole thing was fascinating, if not sordid.

"How did you get divorced so fast?" I asked.

"My daddy made Bill sign a prenup before we got married. I actually forgot all about it. I didn't even read it at the time. Just signed on the dotted line where daddy told me to sign. I was in love. Apparently, the agreement said that if Bill agreed not to contest the prenup, then he got ten-million dollars. If he contested it, he got nothing. I had my attorney offer him twenty and he took it."

"Probably smart on his part," I said. Mostly being supportive. My friend was worth several billion dollars. An extra ten million was like change in most people's pockets.

"And you're married already?" London said, with a level of incredulity behind the voice. Although, I saw a ring on her finger as well. The last time we met three months ago, she wasn't dating anyone. I was certain we'd hear the whole story before our meals were delivered.

Trista flashed her rock. Not that she needed to. The sun glistened off it and was blinding my eyes since I was sitting across from her. Good thing I was wearing sunglasses. That and the glasses covered the dark bags under my eyes that makeup didn't cover from three straight months of crying myself to sleep at night.

The crying was taking a toll on my eyes. The ones Mark said were my best feature. Along with my smile. He liked my hair too. At one time or another, he mentioned just about every one of my body parts was my best feature.

I miss him.

Trista was proud of her ring, even though she was probably the one who paid for it. Sounded like her husband couldn't afford such extravagance. Turns out there was more to the story than that.

"After my divorce was final," she said, "I had to get away. So I went on a cruise. That's where I met Jose. He was a lounge singer on the cruise ship. It was love at first sight."

"You didn't even know him," London said.

She waved her hand dismissively. "I gave him a big tip and he thanked me by coming back to my cabin and . . . well let's just say that we got to know each other pretty well that night."

She was blushing as she said it. At least it seemed like it since her already red cheeks from all the rouge that competed for dominance on her face.

"We got married the next day. Right on the cruise ship. The captain married us."

"Good heavens!" Rhea said. "I hope you got a prenup."

"We aren't actually married," she said sheepishly. "It wasn't official. It was only symbolic. The captain couldn't actually marry us. And we didn't have a license. Or do the blood work."

"Where is Jose now? Did he come back with you?" London asked.

"I'm working on getting him a visa. My attorney said it could take several months to a couple of years. I fly down on the weekends to see him."

"Are you going to get married for real?" I asked.

"Heavens no. I'm enjoying the single life too much. He's cute and all, but he's not marriage material."

But you're wearing a fifty-thousand-dollar wedding ring.

It might've cost a hundred grand for all I knew. While I didn't condone the shacking up, I preferred that over her jumping into a marriage with a man she barely knew, who was probably ten years younger than her.

"Page, is your divorce final?" Trista asked, clearly determined to change the subject off her embarrassment.

"Almost."

She smiled deviously. "There's one more issue to be resolved."

"What's that?"

This oughta be good.

"The House of Gloria."

"What about it?"

"I'm demanding he give it to me."

"Why would you want it?"

"I don't. But I don't want his daughter to have it."

"Don't you think you should just walk away?" I said, not sure why I stuck my nose into it.

"My attorney thinks I have a good shot of getting it. After all, I ran the place for years. It was mine."

"You hated it." I said.

"That's beside the point. And remind me not to call you as a witness."

I'd prefer that as well.

"I would think you'd want to put all that behind you," London said.

"I was always in Gloria's shadow. Walter loved her way more than he ever loved me. I want to take it away from him."

"That sounds vindictive."

"That's what I'm good at."

"A woman's scorn."

"Exactly!"

"What are you going to do with it once you have it?" I dared to ask.

"Close it down. Right after I paint over that picture of Gloria on the wall."

It seemed like she wanted to offer more information and it also seemed like the group wanted to ask more questions, but no one said anything. The best thing to do was to change the subject. Move on to the next relationship train wreck story, which I'm sure was coming.

"What about you London?" I asked. "I see you have a wedding ring on your finger as well."

"Engagement ring. Although, we're practically married. I'm at his place every night. It's a lot nicer than my place."

"You live in a mansion!" I exclaimed.

I'd been to her house. I could fit ten of mine in it.

"He's a wealthy business tycoon. He started a software company out of college and sold it for seven hundred million dollars. He spends his money on houses and cars. Otherwise, he's as frugal as a hotel maid."

I'm not sure what that meant. Or why she thought hotel maids were frugal.

"How did you hook your claws into him?" Page asked, jokingly.

"We met at an art gala. One of my girlfriends was displaying her work. In walked Richard. Somebody introduced us. I don't even remember who. He said he was looking for a house. I told him I was in real estate. He bought the first thing I showed him. A ten-million-dollar beach house. Yada. Yada. Yada. The rest is history."

"He sounds amazing."

"You're all invited to the wedding. It's at the beach house. I'll send you an invitation."

I looked around the table. It was either my turn to talk, or Rhea's. I put in a preemptive strike.

"What's new with you Rhea, on the dating front?" I asked.

"I am *actually* married."

"Married!"

"Yep. I met an actor. I went on an audition, and he was in the room. Up for a different part."

"Is that Billy?" London asked.

"Goodness gracious no. Billy was two guys ago."

"Girl, you change men more often than I get my hair done."

"This is the last time. Jim is the one this time. He's my soulmate."

I'd lost track how many times she had said that about a guy. She was the most promiscuous in the group. Which was saying a lot.

"How come we weren't invited to the wedding?" London asked.

"It was a spur of the moment thing. We were in Vegas. We walked by a wedding chapel, and he made a reference to it. The next thing I know, we're married. Although ... I was a little drunk. Okay. Maybe a lot drunk. I don't really remember it. But I have the video to prove it. We are legally married."

She seemed proud of her marriage for some reason. It seemed like I had less and less in common with these ladies every time we got together. I still enjoyed it though. They were my friends.

The Bible says not to judge. Which is hard to do sometimes, but I had to keep reminding myself of the admonition.

I wouldn't be supportive, but I wouldn't condemn them either. The lunch reminded me that I needed to pray for them more often.

Our food came. They had four salads. They were all watching their waistlines. I guess since now that they had boyfriends, or fiancés, or husbands, or whatever the heck they were. Driving home today, I'd have to replay the conversation in my head and see if I could remember who was with whom and their marital status.

Thankfully, they were avoiding asking me questions. I'd rather talk about all their dalliances, than open up about my own struggles.

The last three months without Mark had been hard.

"What about you, honey?" Rhea eventually said as the waiters cleared our plates. She was staring straight at me, so I knew who she was talking to.

"What about me?"

"How are you holding up?"

"As well as can be expected, I suppose. I'm still not used to Mark not being there when I wake up in the morning. He used to make me coffee every day."

"Are you still living in the same house?"

I nodded.

None of them knew about my financial settlement. I didn't intend to say anything. Wasn't supposed to anyway since I had a confidentiality agreement with the school and the insurance company.

"That must be hard."

"It is." Tears were trying to make an appearance. I fought them back with the tenacity of a bulldog.

"I could have moved, but I decided to stay."

The three million dollars did come in. Not as quickly as Dr. Steele had promised. The insurance company required a release of liability. My attorney said we had a potential wrongful death case against the school and the gun manufacturer. Perhaps even the parents of the shooter. I didn't want to go down that road.

"You might get more than three million," my attorney had said, "but after you pay my fees, you might get less. Even if you get a verdict in your favor, it'll be appealed. It could take years before you see a dime."

I didn't have years. I either had to get a job or sell the house. So, I took his advice and signed the release and put the money in the bank. I hadn't spent a single nickel of it. Instead, I decided to stay in the same house and drive the same car.

Mark's car was still parked in the garage. His clothes were still in the closet. I wasn't ready to face those things yet.

"Why don't you find another place?" London asked. "Not that it's any of my business."

I think that's the first time I'd ever heard one of the ladies use that phrase. We considered ourselves close enough that almost everything was our business.

"I thought about it. At first, I dreaded living in that house. I thought it would remind me of Mark."

"Perfectly understandable."

"Now, that's the reason I want to stay. Because it reminds me of him. It makes me feel close to him."

"I see you're still wearing your wedding rings," London said.

"I know. I haven't been able to take them off. I'd feel naked without them."

"How are you going to find another man if you're wearing your wedding rings?" Rhea blurted.

I felt my mouth gape open.

"Rhea Maria!" Page said.

Rhea shrugged her shoulders and twisted her collagen filled lips to the side like she didn't know what was wrong with what she said.

I tried not to be offended but was.

"I don't want to find another man," I said, curtly.

"I know a dozen guys who'd love to meet someone like you," Rhea said.

"I don't think I'm ready—"

Her mouth widened, then her words spilled out, interrupting me. "You should join a dating app. I'll help you set up a profile."

"I'm not ready to date yet."

"It's like falling off a bicycle. You have to get back on it."

"Mark was my first love. He's the only man I've ever been with."

"You're kidding!" Page said.

Her turn to take a shot at offending me.

Then she frowned. "Oh, right. The Christian thing."

"Yes. Mark and I waited until marriage before we had sex. I'm glad we did."

"I think that's sweet," London said.

"I think it's stupid," Page said. "I can't imagine not having sex with a man before I married him. That's like buying a car without test driving it. That's like telling your hairdresser to give you a new hair style without knowing what he's going to do."

I couldn't believe she compared hairstyles to the sin of fornication. *Don't judge.*

"That was our choice," I said, testily. Hoping she'd get the point and drop it. Page and I often butted heads in these conversations. I could see myself saying something I regretted if she persisted.

She did.

"All the more reason to put yourself out there," Page said. "To see what it's like to date more people."

"I know what it's like. By listening to you guys. It doesn't sound like it's much fun."

"Don't knock it until you try it. I like variety. You don't eat the same ice cream every time, do you?"

"Actually, I do. Vanilla."

"This is your opportunity to sow some wild oats. See what you've been missing out on."

"I think I'll pass."

"You don't have to sleep with the guy," Page said. "Go to dinner. Or lunch if that's too intimate for you. Get a feel for what it's like. You might enjoy it."

"Can you drop it?" I said roughly. "I'm not ready to date. And when I do, I doubt I'll be asking any of you for dating advice."

"Ouch. You don't have to get testy. I was just trying to help."

I excused myself and stood up to go to the restroom.

"What did I say?" I heard Page say as I walked away.

"She's still grieving."

"It's too soon to talk to her about dating."

"We can't let her sink into a depression. We've got to get her out of it."

Of all the nerve! I wanted to wring their necks.

After a few minutes to think about it in the restroom, I thought I owed them an apology. They were just trying to help. Even if it wasn't helping.

I didn't owe them an apology, I decided, but I offered one anyway. "I'm sorry," I said, when I returned.

"We're the ones who are sorry," Rhea said. "You take as long as you need."

I wanted to explode again but held my tongue.

As long as I need?

Maybe God could provide someone for me. Someday. I hadn't even thought about it. If he did, he'd have to strike me with a bolt of lightning to get my attention. I honestly hadn't even noticed another man since Mark died. The thought petrified me.

Page couldn't let it go.

"You're a pretty single girl, with a beautiful figure," she said. "You can have any guy you want."

"I don't want any guy. I want Mark." Tears welled up in my eyes. I dabbed at them with the napkin still on the table.

"I know, honey," Trista said, tapping my hand. "It's hard now, but eventually you'll get lonely and will need someone."

"I'm lonely now."

"All the more reason to put yourself out there," Page said. "That's all I'm saying."

"Page, shut up. You're making things worse."

London glared at her. I would've but my watery eyes wouldn't be very menacing.

"What did I say? I'm just trying to help. She needs a little shove is all."

I wanted to shove her over the deck and onto the putting green below.

Fortunately, my phone rang at that moment. The caller ID said it was someone from the university calling me.

I excused myself and walked away from the table.

"Hello," I said.

"Miss Cooper," the familiar voice on the other line said.

"Yes. Dr. Steele. How are you?"

I hadn't talked to her since Mark's funeral.

"I'm well thank you. Did I catch you at a good time?"

I looked over at the table where the ladies were in an animated discussion about something. Probably still talking about me.

"Yes. Now is a good time."

I turned my back to them.

"I was wondering if you could come by my office sometime. We'd like to meet with you."

"Of course."

"Let me look at my calendar," she said. I could hear papers shuffling in the background. "School starts next week so I can't do it then."

I already knew that. Usually, Mark would be busy getting ready for it. Fall was coming and I could already feel the void of no school.

"How about two weeks from Wednesday?" she said. "Say ten o'clock. Check your calendar."

I didn't have a calendar. Every day was pretty much the same with me.

"That's fine."

"We look forward to seeing you then."

I hung up. Puzzled.

Why did she keep saying we?

11

It felt weird walking into Cooper Hall for the first time since it was renamed for my husband and the first time since the shooting. The main sign reflecting the name change hadn't been constructed and installed, but a temporary sign with Mark's name on it was out front. It warmed my heart to see it.

Whatever joy I felt quickly left when I walked through the main doors and into the hallway where Mark was fatally shot. The building was bustling with students as they were between classes. I avoided looking to the left but could see the exact spot out of the corner of my eye.

The administrative offices were upstairs. I scurried up the stairs faster than a bank robber fleeing a crime scene. A prim and proper woman dressed out of the sixties sat behind the reception desk. Behind her Dr. Steele's name was prominently etched on the door. She greeted me warmly.

"They are waiting for you in the conference room. Do you know where it is?"

Who's they?

I'd been asking myself that question for two weeks and still didn't have the answer. I thought about asking, but I'd know soon enough.

The all-business receptionist stood and came out from behind her desk when I hesitated answering her question. I did know but she had already opened the door and had motioned for me to follow her.

We walked across the hall and she opened that door for me. I mumbled a thank you.

My hands were clammy, so I was thankful when Dr. Steele rose to meet me and gave me a hug instead of extending her hand. Two men were in the room as well. Both looked very distinguished. Definitely professors.

Dr. Steele introduced the men. They obediently stood. I had already walked to the opposite side of the conference table, so I wouldn't have to shake their hands.

Two men in suits both had short haircuts, one white and one black, both with coffee mugs and papers sitting in front of them. One had a bow tie. The other a long thin tie that matched his thin frame and wire rimmed glasses.

The room smelled like a science experiment. I felt like a college student called to the student advisor's office. I hoped it was as innocuous as that. I couldn't imagine why people of this stature were taking time out of their busy day to meet with me.

"This is Dr. Ogley and Dr. Zhu," Dr. Steele said. "They are colleagues of Mark and members of the peer review board who considered publishing his article."

"Ahh."

That made sense. I'd thought about that possibility but dismissed it. As far as I knew, Mark's paper was a settled issue.

I nodded coldly. Bristling inside. It wasn't a settled issue with me. If I could legally publish it myself, I would've already done so. My attorney advised me against it, so I took his advice. For now.

Anger was an emotion I'd felt a lot over the last three months. I had a lot of people to be mad at. The shooter. Dr. Steele. The peer review board.

I thought I had forgiven them. My pastor had helped me with it. It reminded me of the question Peter asked Jesus.

"How many times must I forgive my brother?"

"Seven times."

"How is that possible?" Peter had asked.

"Actually, seventy times seven."

The words resonated with me. I had to keep forgiving them. For my own benefit.

Dr. Steele asked if I needed anything.

"Some water, please." My throat felt like I was in the middle of the desert.

That's when I realized a pitcher of water and cups sat right in front of me. I could've poured it myself. Dr. Steele had already taken the initiative and started the process for me.

I gulped it down. Pouring a second cup seemed too awkward, so I set the cup down and put forth a ready look. The two professors had notepads and pencils in front of them. Dr. Steele had a large file.

I felt inadequate since I had nothing other than my purse which I had draped over the back of my chair.

What do I do with my hands?

Stop fidgeting.

"Thank you for meeting with us today," Dr. Steele said warmly.

"Thank you for inviting me. I think."

They chuckled.

"I'm not sure why I'm here. Why do I feel like I should've brought something with me? At least a pen and paper."

Dr. Steele took a notepad from her pile and shoved it in my direction. Along with her pen. She produced another pen for herself by the time I had them in front of me. At least I had something for my hands to do.

I leaned forward in my chair, clutching the pen so hard, my knuckles were turning white.

Dr. Steele smiled. "Don't be nervous. You're fine. I guess I should've explained why we are meeting. So you wouldn't be caught off guard."

That would've been nice.

Had she mentioned the peer review board, I would've known it was about Mark's paper. Maybe it worked out for the better. Had she told me, it would've given the anger two weeks to stew and get really hot.

My throat was parched again, but I didn't dare reach for another drink. My hand that didn't hold the pen was shaking so much, I might spill the whole pitcher on the table. It'd pour cold water on the meeting.

I felt myself smile at the mental pun. Then reminded myself not to let my voice crack when I spoke.

"Let me get right to it," Dr. Steele said. "We have decided to submit Mark's paper for publication after all. With a few changes."

Really?

I wrote *publish paper* on the notepad. Then underlined it twice. For some reason.

"What kind of changes?" I asked.

"The title for one thing."

"What do you want to change the title to?"

Dr. Zhu answered on her behalf. Mark had told me about him. He was the weasely one with the wire rimmed glasses. Mark couldn't stand him. So neither could I. Even though I didn't know him, and he hadn't spoken a word.

"The current title is *The Heart of Pluto: An Alternative Formation Theory.*"

I nodded. Well aware of the title. I knew the paper by heart. Better than any of them probably. They might understand the physics formulas better, but I knew the paper inside and out. Especially the intent of it. Mark talked about it incessantly for two years.

I got annoyed with him sometimes. What I wouldn't give to have another conversation with him about it. Even if he was droning on and on about things that didn't interest me.

Dr. Zhu stared down at his notes. "We have changed the title to, *The Heart of Pluto, The Plausible Case for Life on Planet Pluto.*"

An objection had formed in my throat. I tamped it down. I liked the title just as well as the first one. Maybe better.

"Pick your battles," Mark used to say.

"I like it," I said.

"We do too," Dr. Steele said. "It describes the direction we wanted the paper to take."

"I think that was the direction Mark wanted it to go. He was making a case for life on Pluto."

"Right. We're keeping the basic premise of the theory that a nuclear explosion caused the crater that formed the heart. And that the explosion could've been caused by man."

"It's an interesting theory," Dr. Zhu said.

"Fascinating hypothesis," Dr. Ogley said, speaking for the first time. "Your husband was a brilliant scientist."

"Thank you."

I wasn't sure if they were buttering me up to lead me to slaughter, or we were having a genuine discussion.

"It's not often in our business that we have an opportunity to prove or disprove a theory," Dr. Ogley continued. "Being that we're discussing outer space. Mark's idea to send a probe to the Kuiper Belt and sample the debris has merit."

Strength was rising up inside of me.

"Mark said that you were skeptical."

"We were skeptical that NASA would approve another probe to Pluto," Dr. Steele explained.

That's not what Mark said, but I wasn't going to quibble over the point. They seemed to be on board now.

"If a probe were commissioned," Dr. Steele added, "the debris could provide invaluable information. First, we could determine if the debris came from Pluto. If we found traces of radioactive material in it, then that would prove a nuclear explosion."

Excitement accented the words. It reminded me of Mark. He got that way when he was talking about Pluto. All scientists probably got excited about discoveries.

"If we could find human DNA in the debris, then that would be a game changer. We could effectively prove for the first time that another planet once sustained life."

"That was Mark's idea."

"We didn't fully contemplate the value of it at the time," Dr. Steele said. "That was a mistake."

My heart was softening somewhat. It seemed like she meant it.

"Although, the environment is more conducive to the possibility of a probe," she said. "Mark's death, though tragic, has given him some notoriety. And not just in scientific circles. We think NASA might be more open to a probe now than they would've been back then."

"I spoke to Senator Gloss at Mark's funeral and mentioned funding a probe," I said.

I saw their eyes widen. Like how dare I talk to the senator without their permission.

"He wasn't optimistic at all," I said. "Appropriations are planned years in advance."

"That's not the way to approach it," Dr. Steele said tersely. The first time she'd showed any tension in her face or voice.

"What is the correct way?"

"We need to work directly with NASA. They submit an annual budget to the president. The president submits a budget to congress. Congress sets the budget. They either rubber stamp it or not. Usually, they add their own pet projects to it. The pork. And it swells. They cut some things and add some things to get to a final budget which the president signs into law. What we have to do is get NASA to include our probe in the budget they send to the president."

"How do we do that?"

"Actually, NASA expects us to come up with various explorations. They don't usually accept them, but they ask us to provide them with our ideas periodically. We think by publishing Mark's paper, adding to the publicity surrounding the circumstances that led ... along with his notoriety, and the compelling theories in the paper, we think that NASA might very well approve another mission to Pluto."

Dr. Steele was stumbling over her words. She didn't want to offend me by insinuating that Mark's death was somehow a good thing. I didn't take it that way. I saw it as God working things together for my good, based on Romans 8:28.

"Most people think Mars is the next frontier," Dr. Ogley said. "Been there, done that. But that's where the money's going. More exploration needs to be done on Mars, but we've been there several times. We've only been to Pluto once. The thought of possibly proving once and for all the existence of life on another planet would be the discovery of the century. Maybe of all time."

Dr. Zhu chimed in. "The nuclear angle is also compelling. If proven, it might be the very thing to bring our world to its senses. How instructive would it be to see what can happen to a planet if nuclear weapons are detonated?"

I knew a liberal agenda was in there somewhere. I didn't object to the premise though. Neither would Mark. A nuclear war would destroy the earth.

"Sounds good to me," I said.

I thought I'd bring up the unsaid elephant in the room.

"What about the God angle?"

"What about it?" Dr. Zhu said, a little too roughly for my satisfaction.

"My understanding is that you rejected publishing the paper the first time because Mark wouldn't take it out."

"We don't think it has a place in a scientific paper," Dr. Zhu said.

"Then I guess we are back to square one."

"Why is that?"

"Mark wasn't comfortable taking God out of the paper and neither am I."

"We didn't call you here today to ask your permission to publish the paper," Dr. Zhu said. "We called you here to inform you of our intentions."

I could see why Mark despised him. His manner was terse and condescending.

"You may think that I'm a weak person," I said, pushing back. "That I don't know how to stand up for myself. Don't underestimate me. I've spoken to an attorney. I know my rights."

"The university owns the rights to the paper," Dr. Zhu said.

"It's also Mark's intellectual property. If you're going to make significant changes to it, and it sounds like you are, you can't do so without Mark's permission. In this case, my permission since I am his wife and executor of his estate, in charge of protecting his intellectual property. My attorney feels like significantly changing Mark's paper is something we can keep from happening."

Dr. Steele raised her hand in the air.

"There's no need for this to be adversarial. Calling in attorneys is a bit premature."

"It sounds like you have already decided to publish with those changes."

"The paper is completed and ready for publication," Dr. Zhu said, matter-of-factly.

"So you really don't care what I think. Why did you even call me here today?"

"We do care what you think," Dr. Steele said. "Dr. Zhu misspoke. It's not that we are taking the references to God out completely, we're just not making it the primary focus of the paper. Not in the same way Mark did."

"What does that mean?"

"We are focusing on the scientific element. That will get us the most support in the scientific community and is all NASA will be interested in."

"I understand the need for scientific clarity," I said. "I like the direction you are taking it. Can't you leave in the theory that the heart might not have been formed by accident? That a higher power might be behind it."

"That'd be disingenuous," Dr. Zhu said.

"With all due respect, your name is not the one on the paper. Would it really hurt your sensibilities to let someone else hold that view?"

Dr. Zhu started to speak, but Dr. Steele stared him down.

"No. It would not hurt us to consider God in the paper. In fact, I think it would be appropriate. And true to Mark. Considering how important his faith was to him."

"It was very important."

"So we are agreed."

Dr. Steele wrote something on her pad. All I had on mine was *publish paper* underlined twice.

"How about this?" she said. "What if we added in the footnotes section, Mark's hypothesis that the heart was formed by a higher power? I agree with you Mia. I think that would help with the authenticity of the paper. Keep it true to Mark's intention. It's our way of honoring him and his hard work."

"I think that would be fine."

Dr. Steele was growing on me. She was certainly nice to me right after the shooting and during the funeral. Protecting Mark's reputation by not telling anyone he had resigned and making sure I got my insurance settlement had not gone unnoticed by me at the time. My attorney had said the insurance company might've made an issue about Mark's resignation had they known about it.

"Then you will support the publishing of the paper?"

"Yes."

"Good. It's important to me that you are comfortable with it."

What was I going to do? Like they said, they didn't need my permission. While I threw out the word attorney, I had no intention of suing them. It seemed like the best deal I could get.

"I want Mark to still be listed as the author."

"So do we."

"I want his students mentioned as well. They put a lot of work into it."

"We agree."

"Then let's do it."

"Simultaneously, we are submitting to NASA a plan for another probe," Dr. Steele said. "Complete with estimated costs and what we hope to accomplish."

"Let's hope they accept."

"I think they might."

It seemed like we were done.

A big weight was lifted off my shoulders. I'd been trying to figure out how to publish Mark's paper. I had not been able to come up with anything.

My heart was elated. Mark would be proud of me. I stood up to them. I don't know what difference it made, except that God was still a part of the paper. Maybe only a footnote, but that's all he was to most of these people anyway.

His legacy would grow. It might make a difference in some people's lives.

And how amazing would it be if NASA committed to a probe? If Mark's hypothesis is correct and there used to be life on Pluto, it could be a monumental discovery for our planet.

I can't wait to see what happens.

12

One year after the shooting.

The day started out in a deep depression and ended in an exhilarating high. Everything in between was sheer torture.

Today was the one-year anniversary of Mark's death. It seemed like I'd suffered through a bunch of anniversaries of my own making over the last twelve months.

One week after the shooting. One month. Three months. Six months. One year didn't feel any different than those did.

They were all hard.

Everything was hard. Like standing in dried cement for a year. Thanksgiving. Christmas. New Years. His birthday. My birthday. Our real anniversary.

Valentine's Day!

Ugh.

On the nine-month anniversary, I made myself a promise. Before the calendar struck one year, I was going to clean out Mark's closet. Make the conscious decision to move on with my life.

Whatever the heck that meant.

Everyone kept saying I needed to. So I made a self-imposed dead-line I was determined to keep. Despite my good intentions, I kept putting it off. Today, I had no choice. I had to do it. If I didn't, I might not ever. Everyone was right. My current emotional state was unhealthy.

Besides, God told me to do it.

There's a time to mourn, Ecclesiastes says.

Verse three of chapter three slapped me right across the face.

There's a time to kill and a time to heal.

That one spoke directly to me. Now is the time to heal. The saying is that time heals all wounds. That's not true. It doesn't if you don't let it. If you are stuck in that moment in time, you won't heal.

Our pastor mentioned the same thing in his sermon last Sunday. He said when Moses died, the children of Israel were allowed thirty days to mourn. I don't know if he was making the point for my benefit, but things suddenly made sense. If thirty days was good enough for Moses, then one year was beyond good enough for Mark.

That didn't mean it'd be easy.

When I entered his walk-in closet, I felt a pang of sadness grip my heart like a vise. Mark's clothes were in the exact same spot they were in when he left that fateful morning. The only exception were the clothes in the hamper, which I had washed and folded. I also ironed his shirts and hung everything neatly in its place shortly after the shooting.

For one last time I admired how Mark valued orderliness and neatness. The scientist in him was on full display in his closet. He said on more than one occasion that if a number in the wrong place of an equation was wrong, then the answer would never be right.

An article of clothing out of place to him just didn't seem right.

I handled his clothes like they were worth millions of dollars. It seemed dishonoring to rip everything off their hangers and throw them into a garbage bag. So, I orderly took them off the hangers, one article of clothing at a time. Snuggled each one against my face and chest, then folded them neatly and put them into a box.

The ritual took up most of the morning. Eventually, all the clothes, shoes, and various items in the closet and dresser drawers were all boxed up and in the trunk of my car. Ready to be donated to a charity.

Minus one.

His favorite shirt. The one I hated. He liked to bum around the house in it. It was a sleeveless T-shirt. With numerous holes in it. The N on the front was faded. It stood for University of Nebraska. The state where Mark grew up.

I couldn't get rid of it. When Mark was alive, I tried to throw it away a couple of times. Each time, he retrieved it out of the trash. Right now, I wouldn't take a million dollars for it. Ironic that this was the one item of clothing I wanted to keep.

With the easier job done, I walked with a purpose to his office. Took a moment to sit in his office chair and picture him in it. It had a computer and monitor sitting on the desk, along with a picture of me on the corner. Otherwise, it was as neat as the closet.

In the office closet were a dozen or so boxes. Filled with Mark's papers. Going back to college through his time at UCSD. I might not get to those today. They'd take hours to go through. Deciding what to throw away would be hard.

How did I know what might be important to keep?

As if on cue, my phone rang. Dr. Steele was calling. We had only spoken once since I met with the peer review board in her office, and she told me they wanted to publish Mark's paper. That was only a courtesy call to let me know the article was published. She sent me a copy in the mail, which I appreciated, but didn't bother calling to thank her for.

The article was a hit, based on the reviews on blogs and social media. I'd had several news outlets call me for interviews after it came out. I turned down the television interviews, but did a number of radio and print interviews.

"Dr. Steele, I know why you're calling," I said, when I pushed the accept button on my cell phone.

"Hard to believe it's been one year. It's gone by fast."

"Thanks for remembering. The year has crawled by for me."

"I suppose. Another school year is over. The longer I'm in this job, the faster the school year seems to go."

"How was the year?"

"It went well. The students were upset that we didn't have a Pluto class, though. You know Mark had a waiting list to get into his class."

I chuckled. "That was his favorite class to teach. I don't mind if you start a new class and use the same curriculum. I could get it for you."

"I don't know anyone on our staff who could do it justice. Mark's shoes are too big to fill."

That gave me a thought.

"Would the university be interested in Mark's papers?"

The boxes in his office closet were staring back at me.

"Absolutely, we would."

"I need to go through them, but I can get them to you in a few weeks' time."

"We'd be honored. We have an entire collections and archives department."

"All his work on Pluto is in his boxes."

After the peer review board refused to publish his paper, Mark had angrily boxed them all up.

"I'd like to display some of his works," Dr. Steele said. "Maybe in the lobby when you first walk into the building."

"That'd be wonderful."

I meant it. Not only did it save me time, but it made sense to donate the papers to the school that named a building after him.

An awkward silence ensued.

"I appreciate you calling," I finally said. "That's extremely considerate of you."

"I wanted you to know I was thinking about you."

"I appreciate that."

"Would you like to get coffee sometime?" Dr. Steele said out of the blue.

"Em … Sure."

"Maybe lunch. I'll text you a few available dates."

"I'd like that."

"No agenda. Just a couple of girls getting together to chit chat."

"That'd be nice. I don't get out as much as I should."

"Then let's plan on it."

"Thanks again for calling."

A feeling of satisfaction came over me as I hung up the phone. That must be what moving on felt like.

The relationship with the university had been strained for far too long. Even though there had been no communication, I could feel it. Deep in my heart.

I'm not sure what prompted me to offer to donate Mark's papers to the university, but now that I had, it felt like the right thing to do. I had no reason to hold a grudge anymore. They named a building after him. They published his article. They'd gone out of their way to honor his legacy.

Even if they didn't before he died, that was the past. I had to acknowledge what they were doing now.

The phone call gave me a renewed vigor. It would make it easier to clean out his office and cut down my workload considerably. The boxes would've taken the most time. Now I could go through them over the next couple weeks and pull out anything personal. Everything related to his work could stay in the boxes and the archivist could organize it.

All that was left for me to go through were his desk drawers and bookshelf. At some point, I'd have to go through his computer as well. There were probably items on there that could be put in a digital file and given to the university.

I'd start with the bookshelf first. The only thing visible on the top shelf was a tin box. I'd never seen it before. I strained to reach it. As I pushed it with my hand toward the edge so I could get a better grip on it, the canister fell and landed at my feet spilling the contents on the floor.

When I bent down to pick them up, I realized they were cards and love letters I had given to Mark over the years. I had no idea he had kept all those things.

A sudden rush of emotion caused tears to well up in my eyes. I sat on the floor and gathered them up. Opened one of them carefully and began reading. One by one they brought me back in time. So many memories came rushing back at once.

When I read the last one, I carefully placed them back in the box and closed it. Held them to my chest and cherished them.

I stood to my feet and collapsed into his office chair. Tears ran down my cheeks and I didn't bother wiping them away. This wasn't an anniversary for gifts, but Mark had given me the best gift ever.

Those things meant something to him as well. To the point that he kept them. I didn't see the sentimental side of him that often.

Many times, I wished he'd show more emotions. It took me a few years of marriage to understand that about him. Now, I realized I may have misjudged him. If my husband kept all my cards and letters to him, he must've felt something.

I wondered how often he read them. Did they move him the way they moved me? It didn't matter. The important thing was that they were important enough to him to keep them.

I was important enough to him.

When my knee hit the edge of his desk, I let out a yelp. The vibration caused the computer screen to come on suddenly. Since it was open, I thought I'd look through the saved computer files and see what could be donated to the university.

One file caught my eye. Marked private.

What?

I hesitated opening it. *Why?*

Because of what my friend Page had said at our girl's country club lunch two weeks ago.

"I'm going to start cleaning out all of Mark's stuff," I had said. "I'm finally ready to do it."

Page's mouth flew open like she wanted to say something. We all looked at her.

"I knew a friend who had a friend whose husband died."

"Okay."

"She went through his stuff. Turns out, he was living a double life. He had another wife in another city."

"How did he manage to keep that a secret?" London said.

"I don't know. He had kids with the other lady."

"What a jerk."

"He was a traveling salesman or something like that. He was gone during the week and home on the weekends. That's how he kept the secret from her."

I didn't think anything of it at the time but did now. Page's words were flooding back in my mind.

"She went through his computer and found emails to the other woman," she said. "Along with pictures."

"I don't think Mark could have another wife on the side," I said. "He's home with me every night."

"I didn't mean Mark," Page said. "Of course, he doesn't have another wife. You probably won't find anything."

Seeing the private flag on the file folder gave me pause. I didn't know what to think. My hand sat on the mouse which hovered over the file.

Don't be silly.

I clicked on it. Five file folders appeared on the screen.

What is this?

I opened the first file. The opening line was a research question.

Why do planets exist if they weren't created to support life?
By: Dr. Mark Cooper

Mark was writing another research article. He never mentioned this to me, not once. And he'd been working on it for more than two years. Obviously simultaneously with the Pluto paper.

It had a fully developed table of contents. As I dug into it, I realized that the entire thing was more developed than I first thought.

The five files corresponded with five points in the paper.

1. Introduction

2. Objectives and Assumptions

3. Identification of the Problem

4. Limitations

5. Significance of findings

It took me more than four hours to read all the chapters because I reread them several times.

The primary assumption was that God created the heavens and the earth and all things in it. Including the planets in our solar system. The second assumption was that God made everything for a purpose. Proverbs 16:4 was the reference Mark used to support that assumption.

The identification of the problem in the third file was fascinating. It began with another research question.

Since God made everything for its purpose, what is the purpose of the planets?

Mark went into almost twelve pages discussing how the planets kept the solar system stable. He identified the size, rotation rate, axis tilt, and gravitational pull of each planet. That's when he lost me, with a number of mathematical equations proving how the sun's gravity pulled on the planets while the planets pulled on each other.

In perfect harmony.

Mark referenced the Pluto paper and its research question. How could the heart on Pluto be formed in such a perfect shape by accident? He asked the same question in this paper. How could the planets be in such perfect alignment and stay in perfect harmony unless a higher power was behind it?

Gravity is the glue that holds the universe together, Mark wrote.

The gravitational magnetism between the earth, the other planets, and the sun, prevented the planets from crashing into each other. The other planets in the solar system exerted a gravitational pull on the earth that kept it in perfect alignment and a safe distance from the sun.

Mark calculated what would happen if even one planet was out of alignment. The results were catastrophic. The earth wouldn't even exist. It'd fall out of its orbit and be pulled into the sun.

He then calculated the mathematical odds of all of the planets falling into the exact position to keep Earth safe. He determined it wasn't mathematically possible. The odds were incalculable. That's how improbable it was.

Concluding that a higher power, God, had to be behind the design, he made that the focus of the end of the paper.

"Why are the planets so desolate?" he asked.

He quoted John Ruskin. "Nature is painting for us, day after day, pictures of infinite beauty."

Compared to the other planets, Earth was the most beautiful by far. Mark described the mountains, sunrises and sunsets, the lakes and streams, the flowers in a field.

The other planets are beautiful in their own way. But not like Earth, he wrote.

Then he asked why.

It was an interesting question. The paper had me mesmerized. I could picture Mark sitting at that very desk, pondering those deep questions.

In the last file, Mark began to make his case.

Twenty-three moons and planets in our solar system have water on them.

Water was necessary for life.

Every planet in the solar system has oxygen. Earth is the only one that has breathable oxygen. Why is that? Because Earth has plants.

He wrote something I didn't know. Scientists had concluded that there were more than 5,000 exoplanets that had plant life on them.

Fascinating.

He referenced a study that reached the following conclusion.

There was at least a fifty percent chance that Mars once had the ability to sustain life. That didn't mean it was inhabited, but it was habitable billions of years ago.

Mark made several arguments that the earth wasn't as old as scientists believed. He talked about the unreliability of radiometric dating techniques. DNA mutation rates. Molecular clocks. Dry stuff that I'm sure was fascinating to Mark and other scientists but was way over my head.

His conclusion was that God created the other planets to sustain life. That it was possible, they all once sustained life, but destroyed themselves and that's why the planets were desolate.

My phone rang interrupting my reading. I was almost done anyway.

Ironically enough, Page was calling me.

"Hi dear," Page said. "How are you doing?"

"I'm okay."

I thought it was sweet that she remembered today was the day of the shooting.

"What are you doing?" she asked.

"I'm going through Mark's things. Today's the anniversary."

"How many years were you married?"

She clearly didn't remember. She was at our wedding. She should've remembered it was in January.

"Not our wedding anniversary. One year since the shooting."

"Oh."

"Why are you calling Page? I don't mean to be rude, but I'm kind of in the middle of something."

"Are you sitting down?"

"I am."

"You know my boyfriend's brother's wife. I told you about her."

"The book agent in New York."

"Right. I talked to him about your book idea."

"It wasn't really an idea. We just mentioned it at the country club."

While at lunch, Page said that I should write a book about Mark and the shooting. Open up about how I was coping. I thought at the time that the book would be disingenuous, since I wasn't coping.

Page mentioned that her boyfriend was related to a book agent at one of the big publishing houses in New York.

I hadn't thought any more of it. Until now.

"I remember."

"Anyway, he talked to his brother, who talked to his wife. They are interested. She'd like to fly you to New York to discuss it."

I felt my mouth gape open.

"I don't know, Page."

"It's already settled."

"This is happening so fast. I don't even know how to write a book."

"They have editors and ghostwriters and all that. They like the story. I don't mean like. You know what I mean. I gave them your number. She's going to call you."

"Okay. I don't guess it would hurt to talk to her."

"Exactly."

"Thank you."

When I hung up the phone, God gave me the title of the book.

Heart to Heart.

13

Five years later

The annual convention for the American Christian Fiction Writers (ACWF) was held in St. Louis under the shadow of the arch. I was asked to be the keynote speaker. More than a thousand aspiring and accomplished writers attended the conference each year seeking to improve their craft.

According to the organizer, Jill Fulbright, this was the biggest conference ever. She attributed it to me. Something I still had a hard time believing. It amazed me that anyone even read my books, much less would travel to a convention to hear me speak.

I was scheduled to speak three times. Even though I'd done it many times over the last five years, it still wasn't something I was comfortable doing. The first night of the conference was a question-and-answer session so I'd get a chance to ease into it. The session was more like an interview which made it easier for me.

Jill was the moderator. We sat on stage, just the two of us, staring out over the crowd in the grand ballroom. My picture was on the two massive screens to the right and left of the stage.

As if I wasn't nervous enough, I had to sit through an almost five-minute effusive introduction. It made me uncomfortable to hear her talking about how great I was.

"The lady sharing the stage with me tonight needs no introduction," Jill said. "She's the best-selling author of 49 books. Her first book, *Heart to Heart*, was number one on the New York Times best seller's list."

Jill looked up from her notes and over at me.

"What do you do for an encore when your first book is a New York Times number one best seller?"

I smiled shyly. Then shrugged my shoulders.

"You write 48 romance novels and sell 93 million copies!"

Everyone laughed. Another two facts I still couldn't believe.

After going over my background and general information, she finally said, "Please welcome, Mia Cooper!"

The crowd applauded enthusiastically. I blushed and waved. The applause went on a little longer than I would've liked. At least they remained seated.

Jill waited for the crowd noise to die down, then she looked at me and smiled. She had sent me a list of potential questions, so I basically knew what she was going to ask. I changed positions in my chair, covering my mouth with my hand, and quietly clearing my throat, preparing to speak for the first time.

"Let's get right to it," Jill said. "Your first book, *Heart to Heart*, was written after your husband died in a tragic school shooting at the University of California, San Diego."

I nodded.

"How did you cope after hearing the news?"

I took in a deep breath.

"Honestly, not so well at first. I'm still coping in some ways."

The first answer was easy and rehearsed. The shoulder tension eased somewhat after I got through the first one without stumbling over my words.

"How long were you married?"

"Not that long really. Mark and I met in college."

I shared how we met and the struggles during our first few years together.

"We graduated college at the same time, but I worked to help put him through graduate school. He became a professor at University of California, Santa Cruz. Eventually, he took a position at UC San Diego."

I realized I hadn't actually answered the question.

"We'd been married ten years."

"Where were you when you first learned there had been a shooting at his school?"

I'd wanted to remove that question. It was the most common question I got in these types of interviews. While I knew my answer by heart, it didn't matter how many times I answered it, I could still feel the emotions of that day. Like I had to keep reliving it over and over again.

I reminded myself that this was the first time the people in the room had likely heard my story. Many of them had read about it, but that wasn't the same as hearing me share it. So I did. For their benefit, not mine.

This was my new normal. My ministry. Like it or not, I was a celebrity, so to speak, and people wanted to hear my story. Our story. This was my way of honoring Mark. To step out of my comfort zone and tell everyone what he meant to me.

Jill asked a number of pointed questions after I answered her question. The tension in the room was getting thick. The emotions intense.

I had a standard line I used many times to ease the seriousness.

"I actually liked Mark. That made it harder. Some women don't like their husbands. I liked him."

Everyone laughed.

"He was my first love."

My voice cracked, which took the room right back to a deep emotional level.

"He was your soulmate," Jill said, soberly. Clearly moved with the emotion I was feeling.

"People often refer to their spouses as their soulmates," I explained. "In this instance, it really was true. It felt like I lost a part of me that day."

You could hear a chair squeak outside the ballroom, that's how quiet it had gotten inside the room.

"How did losing Mark affect your faith in God?"

This was what I liked to talk about. God.

"I don't think it did. If anything, it strengthened it. Don't get me wrong. I was in shock. My whole body was numb for months. The whole thing was really a blur. I remember it, but I don't ... if that makes sense. It seems like it wasn't real. Even now. The one thing that was constant was God. He was always there."

"Did you ever get angry at God?"

"Not at all. Disbelief is how I would describe what I was feeling. Not anger."

"Did you ever ask why? Why God?"

I felt courage and faith rising up inside of me. This was why I was here. To bring encouragement to the room that was mostly ladies. A few men were interspersed among the crowd.

"I didn't think it was my place to ask God why. He said he'd work all things together for my good. I trusted that. And it's true. So much good has come from the tragedy."

Jill's lips twisted to the side. I could tell she wanted to ask a question but wasn't sure how to phrase it. So I answered it for her.

"It's not that God caused the tragedy so he could do good in it. I don't think that. Every good thing comes from God. Mark's shooting wasn't a good thing. An evil man was behind it. An extremely disturbed man. What I'm saying is this."

I uncrossed my legs and leaned forward. "Only a good God could take something so horrible and cause so much good to come out of it."

"That's an inspiring way to look at it."

"It's what has helped me get through it."

"There might be someone in the audience who is going through a hard time," Jill said. "What would you say to her?"

"I'd tell her to keep trusting God. He promised to never leave you nor forsake you. It was during my darkest times that I felt God's presence the most. Even if you don't always feel Him, he's still there and he loves you."

The crowd erupted in applause.

"How did you get into writing?" Jill asked. Meaning we'd gotten through the tougher part of the questions.

"That's a book in and of itself," I said, placing a smile on my face. "I have a friend who has a relative in publishing. I flew to New York to meet with her and she was interested in my story. I didn't have an agent or anything at the time. I was naïve to publishing or what it took to write a book. They wanted to use a ghostwriter. I asked if I could take a crack at it first."

"Why did you want to write it?"

"I wanted it to be my words if at all possible. I know what I went through. I thought the readers would be able to feel the disconnect between the words and me if I didn't write it. To be honest, I didn't know how to write. But God was with me, and the words started flowing. Before I knew it, I had 70,000 words on paper."

"And they obviously liked it?"

"They thought it was horrible."

Everyone laughed.

"The editor had a field day with it. Moving this here and editing that. I learned so much through the process."

"The book came out and was a bestseller."

"Shocked the heck out of me."

"They made a movie. How did that come about?"

"It almost didn't. All the major studios turned it down. They said it was too preachy."

I put the word preachy in air quotes.

"I guess I am a little preachy. Anyway, I'm thankful to BeHoldings Studios for believing in me. They decided to take on the project. Almost went bankrupt getting it out there."

"The movie was a huge success."

"It was. At least by faith-based standards. I mean nothing like the action movies that gross a billion dollars at the box office."

"It says here that it cost five million to make but amassed more than $250 million dollars. You must be proud of that."

"I'm still amazed."

"Tell us how you got into writing romance novels set on Pluto."

"My husband Mark was obsessed with Pluto. He was convinced there was intelligent life on Pluto at some point in the past. Before *Heart to Heart* even came out, I got the idea to write our love story, set on Pluto. With fictional character names. It sort of mirrored our marriage and our idiosyncrasies. I never thought it would be published. I wrote it as my own catharsis."

"How long did it take you to write it?"

"Nearly six months. When I finished it, I drummed up the courage to give it to four of my girlfriends to read. They loved it and thought I should send it to my agent."

"And you did?"

"Yes. She loved it."

"And so you sent it to the publisher?"

"She did. She sent it to the same company that published *Heart to Heart* and they turned it down."

Jill's eyes widened. A groan of disbelief went through the crowd.

"I know!"

"So even though you were a New York Times best selling author, you still got rejected!"

"Amazing, isn't it. That should encourage each of you. It's a tough business out there. If you get rejected, don't take it personally. My agent found a small press who took it on. They've published all my books."

"I guess they aren't a small press anymore. Not 93 million copies later. I bet that original publishing company is kicking themselves."

We recently passed a hundred million, but I wasn't going to make the point. Even though it was cool to celebrate that unbelievable milestone.

"After about book ten, the original publishing company actually contacted my agent and tried to get me back, but I turned them down."

"Good for you."

"I'm happy where I'm at."

"So all of your novels are set on Pluto?"

"That's right. I sort of created my own genre. Historical fiction on another planet. Who knew it would be so successful?"

"You mentioned to me that you have a big announcement related to Pluto. Do you want to share that now?"

"That's right, Jill. My husband wrote a scientific article putting forth the idea that Pluto once had intelligent life on it. There is a heart on the side of Pluto."

"I believe we have a photo of it," Jill said.

She motioned to someone and a picture of Pluto and the heart came on the screen.

A murmur went through the crowd.

"Isn't that heart amazing?" I said. "The big announcement is that NASA is going to send a space probe back to Pluto. They're going to run experiments to see if my husband's theory is correct. The launch is in ten days. We are so excited."

***

Later that night

After the main session ended that afternoon, I did a book signing in the convention bookstore. Based on the line out the door, I was going to be there awhile.

Each person would want to take a minute or so to talk to me. About half would want a picture. I hadn't had a chance to eat lunch and was famished. My goal was to average less than one minute per person. A quick calculation in my head told me I wouldn't be eating for a couple of hours, maybe longer.

"I lost my husband, too," the first woman in line said. "You really helped me to get over it. Not over it. Able to move on with my life."

"I understand."

One of the points I made in the book was that losing a spouse wasn't something to get over. It wasn't even something to get through, since you would live the rest of your life without that person, so you're never through it.

It's more about learning to live without them. Accepting reality. Focusing on the present and future, not the past. The first lady took at least two minutes. I didn't have the heart to rush her.

"I love your books so much," the next lady said. "I can't put them down. As soon as a new one comes out, I read it the same day. I need you to write faster."

I laughed. I was already producing a book a month. Tomorrow, I was scheduled to talk about my writing style and give them pointers on how to develop a plot, how to write interesting dialogue, and how to make the characters likable and engaging.

She wanted a picture, so I obliged. It took longer than one minute with her as well. Thirty minutes later, the line of ladies still stretched outside.

The only man in the bookstore was over by my table, looking at the back cover of one of my books.

He's handsome.

Why did that thought pop into my head?

Why did I even notice him? Because he stuck out like the only house on a street with Christmas lights on the roof.

The next lady had tears in her eyes, bringing me back to reality.

"My son passed away last month. My husband died a couple of years ago. I feel so alone."

"Can I give you a hug?" I said, knowing that would add at least a minute to this encounter.

"Ohhhh. I'd love that."

I stood and walked around the table and took her in my arms. Her tears wet my cheek.

"If you keep choosing God, then healing will come. I promise."

I squeezed her tighter. She brushed the tears away when I released her. I walked back around the table and signed her book. Even personalized it for her. I usually only did that when they asked. By that point, I was resigned to the fact that dinner would have to wait. These ladies needed me and had waited in line all this time. I wasn't going to rush them away, because I didn't have the foresight to eat something this afternoon.

"Could someone get me something to drink?" I asked the girl who was a staff person for the bookstore.

A few minutes later, she brought me some water. That'd have to do.

When she walked away, I used the opportunity to look around the room for the handsome stranger. He was no longer at my table. I spotted him at the cashier, purchasing one of my books.

Good. Another paying customer.

He looked like he could afford it. He was sharply dressed in a tailored jacket with a white shirt, no tie, and an open collar. His shiny shoes were free of laces. Some kind of leather loafers. A little graying around the ears. Late thirties, early forties, I guessed.

"I can't believe I'm meeting you!" the next woman in line said, drawing my attention back to the task at hand.

After another half hour, the end of the line was inside the room. My stomach was churning. Shouting for food.

It wouldn't be long if I sped things up.

"It's so nice to meet you," I said to the young girl standing in front of me with her mother. She couldn't have been more than ten years old. "What's your name, honey?"

The girl told me then shyly handed me her book. I opened it and penned my name and personalized it to her.

Her mother handed me her book and I signed it. As I started to hand it back to her, I realized that I had forgotten to look and see which book it was. For my *Heart to Heart* book, I always wrote Ecclesiastes 3:3 under my name. For my romance titles, I simply wrote with love and then signed my name with a black sharpie. Occasionally, I put a heart over the i in Mia, instead of the dot.

The stranger was moving. I could see him out of the corner of my eye.

What's he doing?

Why was he still in the room? It had been at least an hour since I first spotted him.

He was in the line now. With a book in his hand. My heart started racing. I didn't want to meet him.

Maybe if I slowed down and took my time, he'd lose patience and leave. Surely, a man like that had better things to do than get a worthless signature from me.

My stomach wouldn't let me stall. I might faint if I didn't eat something soon. I could feel my energy waning. My blood sugar dropping.

Just my luck, I'd keel over on the spot.

I wonder if he knows mouth-to-mouth resuscitation.

Mia Cooper! What in the world!

I scolded myself like a mother scolds a teenager daughter. I couldn't believe such a thought popped into my head. That sounded like something one of my characters in a book would say.

Eventually, the line thinned.

He was next. I could feel his presence hovering over me. I didn't dare look up and catch his eye.

Why was I so nervous?

The lady before him wanted a selfie. I wanted to walk out of there and say the book signing was over.

I handed the lady the signed copy and she left.

I looked around. The man and I were the only two people in the room other than the cashier at the register. I felt extremely uncomfortable.

The cashier was busy counting money and not paying us any attention at all.

I looked up and smiled. Our eyes met for the first time. He handed me a book. One of the romance novels. That immediately made me suspicious. He wasn't wearing a lanyard which told me he probably wasn't part of the conference.

I knew my audience. Ninety percent were ladies 35 and over.

"I'm the last one," he said.

It seemed like he had orchestrated that on purpose. So we would be alone.

His voice was smooth like a purring engine. His after shave was cool and fresh. It had that end of the day smell. I'd smelled that on Mark many times when he came home at the end of a long school day.

Now that I could see his eyes, he was even more handsome than I first thought. Not movie star handsome. More quarterback of the varsity football team handsome.

His smile displayed perfectly formed teeth, that looked like they had been whitened. I didn't feel pretension though. Only someone who was meticulous and sought perfection in life. Like Mark was about his clothes and about science.

"Saved the best for last," I blurted. Then immediately regretted it.

That was an entirely stupid thing to say.

My stomach growled loud enough for him to hear it, only adding to my embarrassment.

"Should I make this out to anyone in particular?" I asked.

"Collin," he said, flashing his pearly and charming smile. "Two l's."

I wrote the name carefully. Normally, I had good penmanship, unless I got in a hurry. I didn't want to mess this up. I also didn't want him to see my hand twitching from the nervousness.

I handed him his book. He opened it and looked at the signature with approval.

My stomach growled again. Even louder this time. He did notice. It caused him to chuckle and also flash the one dimple on the left side of his cheek.

"I'm starving," I said. "I haven't eaten anything since breakfast."

"Good," he said. "Because I was wondering if I could buy you dinner."

I about fell off my chair. He did arrange this.

Of all the nerve! He really is asking me out on a date.

Did he not see the wedding rings on my finger? Did he not care?

My mind raced back to my question-and-answer session in the main ballroom. I tried to picture the crowd to remember if he was in there. If he was, then he'd know my story. That I wasn't married.

I think I would've noticed him.

Regardless, did he think I wouldn't notice the wedding rings on his fingers?

14

My face flushed when the handsome stranger asked me to dinner. It turned to anger when I remembered he had a wedding ring on his finger and had ignored the rings on mine. I should be flattered, I suppose, but it went against all my sense and sensibilities.

I sound like a Jane Austen novel.

While I wanted to give him the benefit of the doubt, it was hard to overlook the obvious.

Nevertheless, I was the guest of honor at the convention. A certain decorum should be expected from me. He could be attending the conference. Perhaps he was even on staff. He had purchased one of my books, which made him one of my customers.

Even if he was married, asking me to dinner wasn't a crime. This was a Christian conference. Perhaps his intentions were truly above board.

But I knew when a man was interested in me and asking me out.

How do you know that?

You haven't been asked out since college.

A woman knows these things.

The debate raged in my head and was giving me a headache to go along with my stomach which ached for food.

That's when I realized I hadn't actually answered his question.

"I was wondering if I could buy you dinner," he had asked, some thirty seconds ago.

The words had lingered over the table for so long, they were growing as stale as a book stored in a basement. At that point, I was past the point of seeming awkward and had crossed the line to rude.

"How are you enjoying the conference?" I asked, deciding to ignore the question altogether. I didn't know if I was pretending not to hear it or acting too afraid to answer. Either way, I felt foolish.

"I'm not part of the conference," he said. "I'm in town on business."

"Hmm."

That told me a lot. He didn't know I wasn't married.

Having signed his book, standing to my feet I took my purse off the back of the chair and slipped it over my arm. Maybe he'd get the hint and I'd never see him again.

He didn't seem to. He stood there smiling like he was waiting for an answer.

Now I was bristling inside. Obviously, he was a hound on the lookout for his next woman to tree. I could spot that kind of man a mile away. Men like that were a dime a dozen in my novels.

"I was roaming around the hotel, and I saw all the people in the ballroom," he said. "I saw you on stage and I stopped to listen. I was fascinated and wanted to meet you."

And now you're stalking me.

"Nice to meet you, too. If you'll excuse me, it's been a long day."

So he may know I'm not married if he heard my story.

Didn't matter. I walked toward the door and out of the room and began striding down the hall with a purpose. The wide hallway was empty. Even the vendor booths were closed for the evening. The writers were all in breakout sessions. It had to be getting close to eight o'clock.

The stranger followed me out and was now keeping pace beside me.

"I was touched by your story," he said.

Whatever. Now leave me alone.

We came to the elevators. He was still by my side. I pushed the up button. I needed to go to my room and get changed into something more comfortable, then make a beeline for the restaurant downstairs.

I wasn't sure I felt comfortable getting on the elevator with him. Alone. I didn't really have a choice. The elevator doors opened, and I stepped inside. He followed me in.

Much to my dismay.

I started to push the button to my floor but thought better of it. I didn't want him to know which floor my room was on. Instead, I hit the lobby button which was down. Even though I had hit the up button when I called for the elevator. Fortunately, the elevator didn't go up or I really would've felt foolish.

"I'm sorry for your loss," he said. He seemed sincere.

Serial killers often seemed sincere to their victims. I'd seen documentaries on killers. People that knew them were almost always shocked.

"Thank you."

That's all I knew to say.

Now that I thought about it, how did he know I didn't remarry? Did I mention it in the session? I couldn't remember. Again, didn't matter. He was married and was a cad for even suggesting dinner with another woman.

The elevators were fast and thankfully reached the lobby quickly. I exited. He was still following me. I turned to face him.

"Collin, it was nice to meet you. I hope you have a pleasant evening."

"What about dinner? You never said yes or no."

Is it not obvious? Are you that clueless?

I bit my tongue. Trying not to be completely rude.

The restaurant was right across from the elevators. I ate there the night before when I arrived at the hotel. It had a bar and a large number of televisions with various sporting games going and the food was good.

A line had formed out into the hallway. Just my luck. I took a place at the back of the line.

Collin stood next to me.

How am I going to get out of this? Did he think we were going to eat together?

"Let me buy you dinner," he implored. "I really have no ulterior motives. I have some questions for you."

Yeah right.

Questions like, would you like to come to my room for a nightcap?

He saw me hesitate. Not because I was considering it, but because I wasn't sure the best way to get out of it. I wanted to put him in his place. I had no experience dating, but I also didn't have any experience in rebuffing advances.

Then I felt like I heard a still small voice tell me to accept the invitation.

Seriously, God?

"Okay," I said, before I had a chance to really see if it was the Holy Spirit or the enemy tricking me.

I immediately regretted it. I couldn't believe I had actually accepted the invitation. Impulsively.

Perhaps it's a ministry opportunity.

Missionary dating! With a married man!

"Let's not eat here," he said. "The line is too long."

I wasn't leaving the hotel with him.

"There's a wonderful steak house on the other side of the lobby. Have you ever eaten there? It's fantastic."

I saw it when I checked in the night before.

"I haven't. It looks expensive."

There was a restaurant by the same name in San Diego. My country club girlfriends went there all the time. Mark and I never did since we were living on a teacher's salary.

I was independently wealthy now and still hadn't eaten at any place remotely fancy. With my books and movie deal and the insurance settlement, I had well over ten million dollars in the bank, but I actually spent less every year than I did when Mark was alive.

Eating out was not something I did often, but when I did, it was some kind of fast-food salad or Chinese place.

He took my arm and led me toward the other end of the hotel.

Hey!

Part of me liked his confidence. A bigger part of me was offended that he had touched me.

Neither of us said anything as we crossed the lobby to the restaurant. Thankfully, he took his hand off my arm, so I didn't feel like a dog on a leash.

"A table for two," Collin said to the host who was wearing a suit.

It is fancy.

Now I really wish I had gone to my room to freshen up. Although I had consumed half a packet of breath mints throughout the day, my mouth tasted like the inside of a chicken coop. I probably smelled like I'd spent the day working in a petting zoo.

I certainly wasn't adequately prepared for a date.

Was this a date?

Why did I even think that? I hoped he wasn't thinking I was interested in him.

The host told us to follow him. Collin motioned for me to go first.

The inside of the steakhouse smelled of prime rib and leather. Dimly lit, chandeliers hung from the ceiling casting many-faceted shadows. The walls were dark cherry-stained mahogany wood, the floor a rich carpet that was soft under my feet.

The maître de led us to a booth in a semi-circle shape. I would've preferred a table or a booth that separated us. Less intimate. I scooted in on my side, so we were across from each other. He made no effort to move toward the center which caused me to breathe a sigh of relief inside.

Maybe he sensed my uncomfortableness. Maybe he was moving slowly. Trying to get me to let my guard down.

Not happening, buddy!

I didn't actually know if a move was coming. My imagination was running wild. As was my heart, which was fluttering and beating much too fast.

The soft candle on the table provided a nice ambiance and, normally, I would've enjoyed it. But it felt way too romantic.

Within seconds of sitting down, a waiter in another suit and bow tie filled our water glasses. A second waiter behind him placed a menu on the table in front of me and two in front of Collin. A thick leather-bound monogrammed version of the fanciest menu I'd ever seen.

I opened it slightly, then closed it when I saw the price of a steak.

"Welcome. Is this your first time?" the waiter asked.

I nodded.

This is my first time to have dinner with a man who wasn't named Mark.

"It's not my first time," Collin said.

I bet it's not. I could imagine he had done this many times.

I wondered if he had ever been caught.

"Can I start you out with a glass of wine or a cocktail?"

Collin looked at me. I shook my head.

"I'll have iced tea," I said.

"Water for me."

"Can you bring us some bread?" I asked. Something in my stomach might settle my nerves and save me a trip to the emergency room.

"Coming up," the waiter said.

Collin handed the waiter the beverage menu. Someone was behind him waiting to put hot bread on the table.

I devoured a piece in a couple of bites, hardly taking time to enjoy it.

I moaned approvingly, then realized how that might've sounded. I wasn't that kind of woman who would flirt and lead him on and then reject him at the last minute.

Rejecting him up front was my intention. *Right now.*

It gave me the impetus to be direct. The sooner I knew his intentions and set them in alignment with mine, the easier it'd be to enjoy the evening.

"I couldn't help but notice the wedding ring on your finger," I said, curtly.

He looked down at it. Then twirled it around his finger a couple of times. Clearly nervous.

"I know. My wife died three years ago from a long illness. I haven't been able to take it off. Is that weird?"

I searched his demeanor to see any hint of lying. If anything, what I saw was heartbreaking. He was still grieving. His eyes were filled with deep sorrow.

"Ahh."

Maybe this was why God wanted me to meet with him. I could help him. I suddenly felt guilty for judging him.

Still, instinctively, I looked around the restaurant to see if any of the conference attendees might be in the restaurant. I didn't want to give the appearance of impropriety. For some reason, it still felt inappropriate, even though we were both single.

"It's not weird," I said. "It's been five years for me. I haven't been able to take mine off either. I'd feel naked without them."

Why did I use the term naked?

I was so out of my element.

"Tell me about your wife," I blurted, trying to cover up my previous remark.

"Martha . . ." his voice cracked, "was an amazing woman. We met when we were fifteen. We lived on the same street in Denver. Her parents moved there when I was sixteen. The first time I saw her, I said, 'God, I'm going to marry that girl.' And I did."

So he knows God.

"We were friends first. Then dated, sort of. It was awkward. We were kids and really didn't know much about love."

"That's the best way to start a marriage. With a friendship."

"As soon as she turned eighteen, we were married."

"What did her parents think about that?"

"Surprisingly, they were supportive. Everyone knew we were supposed to be together."

"Do you have any kids?"

"One daughter. She's in college now. University of Colorado in Boulder."

"You don't look old enough to have a daughter in college."

"I'm forty-one. We had Sandy a couple of years after we married."

He pulled out his wallet and showed me a picture.

I laughed.

"I didn't know people carried pictures in their wallets anymore," I said. "I thought everything was on phones."

"I'm a little old fashioned, I guess."

"She's beautiful."

"She's my pride and joy."

"I can see why."

He was so nice and sincere. If it was all an act, then he was good at it.

"Do you still live in Denver?"

"Yes."

"What do you do for a living?"

"I'm a refrigeration salesperson. You know, commercial industrial products."

"That sounds interesting. Do you like Denver?"

I realized I was peppering him with questions. Perhaps to see if there was a flaw in his story. More likely to keep the conversation about him and not me.

"I love it."

"Even the winters?"

"Especially the winters. I love skiing. Mountain biking. Hiking. I actually water skied, and snow skied on the same day."

"Wow! How did you do that?"

"Snow skiing is only an hour from Denver. My friends and I skied in the morning and water skied in the afternoon. I wore a wetsuit of course. The water was too cold to go in unprotected."

"That sounds like fun. Actually, it doesn't. I'm not much of an athlete. I don't even go to the gym. I spend most of my days behind a computer. My fingers are in world-class shape though."

I waved my long skinny fingers in the air. Someone once told me I should learn to play the flute. That I had perfect fingers for it.

"I'm in pretty good shape," he said. "For an old man. I don't go to the gym either. I prefer to be doing something when I'm exercising. Like riding a bike. Or skiing. Or playing racquetball. Someday, I hope to do some hang gliding or parachute out of a plane."

"I admire risk taking. Even though I'd never do something like that myself. I'm one of those who puts my foot in the water to test it out before I go in."

"I'm a jump-right-in kind of guy."

"Sounds like it."

Over the next hour, we had a wonderful conversation and the best meal I've had in my entire life. I ordered the filet. He ordered the prime rib. I wanted to pass on the salad because it cost extra. He must've sensed it because he insisted.

"You're starving. Get a salad. It takes a little while for the steak to come out."

I'm glad I did order it. The Caesar salad was delightful and between the bites and conversation, I barely noticed that the uncomfortableness of eating with a strange man was fading.

Along with the filet, I ordered steamed broccoli, and he ordered the julienne potatoes. With caramelized onions, fresh thyme, and soaked in garlic butter. That told me he didn't intend on trying to kiss me. *Good thing.*

I'm sure he'd pass out from one whiff of my breath by that point.

He also insisted on ordering the crème Brule even though I was stuffed. We shared it, which was fine since I was growing more comfortable with him. He really seemed like a good guy and a perfect gentleman. Still madly in love with his wife. He mentioned her several times.

The crème Brule was heavenly. A vanilla custard topped with fresh berries.

"I might not ever eat again," I said, as I sat my spoon down on the table.

The waiter brought the check, so I brought up what it seemed like he was avoiding.

"You said you had some questions for me."

Collin was suddenly uncomfortable for the first time. Fidgeting even. Moving the custard around with his spoon. Staring off in the distance. His brow furrowed and I sensed he wanted to deepen the tenor of the conversation.

"During your talk earlier tonight, I heard you say that you need to channel your pain into a purpose. What did you mean by that?"

"That's a good question. It's like my books. The characters in my novels are often flawed. Sometimes, they've gone through a trauma in their lives. Writing is a way for me to channel my pain and express it through my characters."

"So, you poured yourself into your work. That doesn't really help me."

"Not at first really. I didn't start writing until more than a year after Mark's death. Although, it hardly seems like work to me. I love writing novels."

"Forty-nine books in five years. How do you find the time?"

"I'm not a morning person. My husband was. Now I get up when I get up. Have my coffee. Do housework. Pay the bills. Sit on the porch and read my bible. Whatever. After lunch, I sit down at the computer, and I write. I try to finish ten thousand edited words by the end of the day."

"That sounds like a lot."

"It is. I write six days a week. Eight to ten hours a day. I can complete a novel in six days."

"That's amazing."

I shrugged. "I suppose."

"That doesn't leave time for much of a social life."

"That's true. But I haven't noticed."

"I work too much as well."

I didn't say I worked too much.

The remark struck me the wrong way.

"After Martha died, I had Sandy to raise. So that took up a lot of my time."

"I can imagine."

"Once she went off to college and the house was empty, I pretty much went into a shell. I'm home every night by six. Sit down in front of the couch and watch television. Make myself a prepackaged dinner in the microwave. Watch the clock until it hits eleven. Then I make myself go to bed. I feel like I'm in an emotional rut."

He looked at his expensive looking watch.

"If I wasn't with you right now, I'd be in my hotel room. Watching television. And the clock. Waiting until it was time to go to bed. Even then, I don't sleep very well."

"You should get involved in a church."

"Oh I am. I go to church and to a life group. But everyone in the group is married. Martha and I went to that group before she died so I know everyone. They try to be supportive, but they don't understand what I'm going through. The loneliness I feel."

That's sad.

I wanted to give him a hug.

He must've realized the mood had grown too somber. Perhaps, he was feeling too vulnerable. His tone and manner changed noticeably.

"How have you handled getting back in the dating scene?" he asked, out of the blue.

"I haven't really. This is the first time I've shared a meal with someone who wasn't one of my girlfriends."

"Why not?"

I suddenly felt really uncomfortable. Like it wasn't any of his business.

"I don't have the time."

"Couldn't you make the time?"

Now I was bristling on the inside. Fortunately, I was able to keep it from appearing on my face. Or at least he didn't notice.

"Like I said, I write ten hours a day. Usually in the evenings. There's no time for dating."

"That sounds like an excuse more than a reason."

"I beg your pardon."

"Is anyone making you write ten thousand words a day?"

"Well ... no. No one is making me."

"Then why do it?"

"I love what I do."

"I get that. What I mean is—"

"Yeah. Exactly what do you mean!"

He hesitated.

"Go ahead. Say what you want to say. I'm a big girl. I can handle it."

Why was I so mad? It seemed totally an overreaction to a conversation that was going so well.

"Okay. You could write five thousand words a day instead of ten. Put a book out every two weeks instead of every week."

"I don't want to do that."

"That's my point. We do what we want to do."

"Maybe I don't want to date anybody. I'm perfectly content with my life."

"You said we need to channel our pain into a purpose. It sounds like maybe you are avoiding dealing with your pain."

"Are you a psychiatrist now?"

The waiter appeared to take the check. I snatched it up before Collin could.

"Can you make it separate checks please?" I said roughly.

"I told you I was buying."

"I can afford to buy my own meal."

"I'm sure you can. That's not what I meant."

"Never mind," I said to the waiter. I produced a credit card and handed it to him. Put the whole amount on my card.

"You don't have to—"

"I insist."

The waiter hesitated, then walked away.

"Have I offended you in some way?" he said, after the waiter was out of earshot.

"No. I'm fine."

Now I could tell he was mad. His eyebrows narrowed.

"You don't seem fine. All I was trying to say is that maybe you are living vicariously through your characters to avoid feeling the emotions in real life. It's understandable if you are. It's perfectly normal to want to avoid men. But unhealthy."

"Why? Because I don't want to jump in bed with every guy that comes along. Or I'm not in any hurry to get married. I don't expect you to understand. I love my husband. I'm still committed to him. I don't see anything wrong with that."

The tears were trying to escape my eyes. I fought them back.

The waiter returned with the receipt and my credit card.

"Maybe that's why you are so good at writing romance novels," he said. "That's how you express your emotions. That's all I'm saying."

I told myself to calm down.

Until he added, "Which makes you emotionally unavailable to everyone else. Especially those of the opposite sex."

My mouth gaped open.

I was speechless.

I signed the check roughly. It gave me pause when I saw how much it was. Well worth paying for it though, for the effect.

I put the credit card back in my purse and scooted out of the booth. Stood to my feet and towered over him.

"It was very nice to meet you, Collin. I wish you all the best."

I didn't even offer my hand for him to shake.

Before he could respond, I twirled adeptly, and stormed out of the restaurant.

I couldn't remember the last time I was that mad at someone.

15

The next morning

It's so easy to lie. Even for a Christian.

"How did you sleep?" Jill asked me, the next morning at breakfast.

"Wonderfully," I said, lying through my teeth.

I tossed and turned all night. The dinner with Collin played in my head most of the night like a B movie. So many things I should've said to him popped into my mind. Why couldn't I have thought of those things at the time?

How dare he analyze me!

He came to me wanting help. Before I knew it, he was trying to tell me what was wrong with me.

That takes a lot of nerve. We had just met. Right when I was beginning to like him and let my guard down, he ruined everything. And it cost me more than two hundred dollars when I paid for dinner.

Once I was able to put the emotions aside, I decided there was no malice behind his words. More of a condescension. Like he was talking down to me. I felt vulnerable and exposed even though his words weren't true.

Beyond that, I felt the competing emotions of relief and guilt that I had left him there in that manner. Relief that I'd dodged a bullet. Guilt that I had been rude. It wasn't like me. Surely, I was more mature than that. Running away like a wounded rabbit, simply because he said something that hurt my feelings. That kind of behavior was beneath me.

Collin was the reason I didn't date. He seemed like a nice guy at first. But no one was ever going to live up to Mark's standards. I was closing in on forty. The men my age were either divorced with kids or single with commitment issues. Or the type of guy no woman would ever want to marry.

Regardless, it was time for me to pull it together. I had a session to teach that morning. Last night had been a painful lesson. My life was fine just like it was. I didn't need a man to be fulfilled.

The room was abuzz with writers eager to learn. I stood at the front behind a lectern with a microphone in one hand and a remote in the other connected to a PowerPoint presentation. Today's teaching was carefully laid out. I knew exactly what I was going to say. I'd taught this same class several times before at other writer events.

I always started with jokes.

"You're here because you want to know what you need to do to make a living as a writer. Well . . . that's difficult to put into words."

They all laughed.

"How do you make a small fortune writing? You start with a large fortune."

When the laughter died down, I said, "Do you know what the difference is between a writer and a large cheese pizza?"

"No."

"A pizza will feed a family of three."

Sad, but true. I went on to explain that the average book sold 75 copies. The average indie writer spent five hundred to a thousand dollars to publish a book. Most made less than a hundred dollars in total sales.

Some in my audience were traditionally published by a publishing house and received advances. However, between one and two percent of all books were ever actually published. Most people would never make any money at their writing.

I said all that not to discourage them. Rather, I wanted to encourage them to write anyway.

If I could help them become a better writer, then I wanted to. If they were able to make a living out of it, all the better. If all of them could learn to write for the love of it, then I will have accomplished my goal in teaching this class.

"Let me start with my writing process," I said, after a few opening remarks. "I want to get that out of the way, so we can discuss character development and writing an engaging story."

I pushed a button and a slide appeared.

"Point number one. The key to writing is writing."

Everyone laughed again.

"I write six days a week. Ten thousand words a day."

The entire room groaned.

"I know. Not everyone can do that. I don't have kids or a husband to take care of."

A pain shot through my heart when I mentioned Mark.

Collin suggested I should write five thousand words a day and use the rest of the time for dating. If I was still married to Mark, I would write less. It didn't make sense to me to sacrifice my career and write less to date some random strangers I don't have a future with.

Men like Collin. A waste of time and mental energy. I'd lost a night's sleep and two hundred dollars because of him.

The man was obviously still in my head.

"You don't have to write ten thousand words a day," I said to the group, getting back to the task at hand. "Write what you can but write something every day. Even if it's only one paragraph. Eventually, that paragraph will be two paragraphs. Then a whole page. Before you know it, you'll have a chapter written."

A woman raised her hand.

"Do you outline your books before you start writing?"

"That's a good question. I'm what they call a pantser. I write from the seat of my pants. I find out what happens in my books at the same time the reader finds out."

"How do you know what to write?"

"I can hear the dialogue in my mind. I can picture the scene."

I explained my process. How I edited as I went along. Used a writing software to keep track of characters. Sometimes I closed my eyes and envisioned my characters talking to each other.

"There's nothing wrong with producing an outline if that works for you. Are there any other questions?" I asked.

No one raised a hand, so I said, "Now, I'm going to give you the rules of writing. Rule number one, there are no rules."

They all laughed. It took a few seconds to get them quiet.

"I break all the so-called traditional rules. I may use "it was" in a sentence. I may end a sentence with a preposition. I might even say asked instead of said after dialogue. A lot of my sentences don't have verbs in them. That's how people talk. In incomplete sentences. Like what I just did now."

Most of them were furiously writing, so I slowed down.

For fifty minutes, I gave them practical tips on writing, then we took a ten-minute break. When we came back, I began discussing character development.

During the break, I went to the restroom. Not that I needed to. I wanted to see if Collin was lurking. He mentioned the night before that he had an early flight to catch. I didn't see him and assumed he was on a plane back to Denver. *Good riddance.*

I felt a little pang of regret at the mean thought. In some ways, it would've been nice to have the opportunity to apologize. Not because I did anything wrong, but because I didn't like treating people that way. Even if they deserved it.

Knowing he was on a plane and out of my life forever did help me focus on the class.

"Introduce your main character right away in the book," I said. "Preferably in the first chapter. By name."

I looked down at my notes. The outline of my points was in my notebook, but I knew them by heart. If I ever forgot them or lost my place, all I had to do was look at the screen and go to the next slide.

"Let readers get to know your characters. Make your characters human. Give them a flaw. Make them vulnerable."

I paused to let everyone who was taking notes catch up.

"Draw on your own experiences in character development. Let the characters become real to you. Let you become real to them."

That's when it hit me right between the eyes. I felt myself shake my head from side to side. A wave of emotions washed over me like a washing machine cycle drowned the clothes.

Isn't that what Collin said last night?

No!

That's exactly what he said.

The conversation was etched in my mind. A little man on my shoulder was making the same argument Collin had made the night before.

"You are living vicariously through your characters to avoid feeling the emotions in real life," Collin had said.

That's not what I'm doing.

That's exactly what you are doing, the little man insisted.

Shut up! I am not.

I'd waited too long to make the next point in my presentation and the crowd in the room was collectively staring at me.

I had to look down at my notes to find my place.

"Give your characters a past," I said. "Let the reader know what makes them who they are today."

The conversation from the night before rushed to the forefront of my mind again.

"It sounds like maybe you are avoiding dealing with your pain," Collin had said.

That's what really made me mad and the reason I left.

The little man was relentless.

You never got over your past. You spend ten hours a day with your characters rather than real people.

I ignored him.

"Make your characters human," I said. Then realized I had already made that point. Some people wrote it down a second time giving me time to regroup. Also time for Collin and the little man to pepper my thoughts.

Is anyone making you write ten thousand words a day? Collin said.

It sounds more like an excuse than a reason, he had said accusingly.

"Give your character a past," I said.

I'd already said that as well. To save myself, I said, "I repeat it because it's important."

If I could, I'd skip through that point for obvious reasons. My past was still painful. But I decided to expound on it because it was really important to the writing process.

"It's called a backstory. You've all most likely heard that term. Don't give your readers all the backstory at once. Spread it out through your story. Let the past unfold slowly."

That's what I'm doing, Collin. I'm taking my time getting over my backstory.

Collin was right in my ear with his rebuttal.

"All I was trying to say is that maybe you are living vicariously through your characters to avoid feeling the emotions in real life. It's understandable if you are. Avoiding men."

I'm not avoiding men.

My main characters are often men.

"Maybe that's why you are so good at writing romance novels," Collin had said. "That's how you express your emotions. Which makes you emotionally unavailable to everyone else."

The little man's turn to berate me.

You deal with your emotions through your characters. That way you can control them.

I decided to ignore the little man and address Collin.

So what if I didn't want to reveal every emotion to you, Collin, the first time we met. That doesn't mean I'm emotionally unavailable. I'll open up when I meet the right guy.

You are emotionally unavailable, the little man said.

The only thing I knew to do was ignore them and continue teaching the class. They were distracting me.

"Give your character an internal and an external conflict," I said, making the next point in the presentation as emphatically as I could. The problem was the pauses between points to let people write them down. The silence in the room allowed for the noise in my head to continue.

"I feel like I'm in an emotional rut," Collin had said. "I'm having a hard time dealing with the loneliness since Sandy went to college."

At least he's being honest, the little man chimed in. *I can't say that about you.*

"Writing is a way for me to channel my pain and express it through my characters," I said out loud to the class.

Did I just say that?

It wasn't in my notes. Then I remembered. Collin said that to me the night before. That's why it was still stuck in my head.

At that point, I thought it best to take another break. A longer one. I needed to end the session and go back to my room to regroup. The whole thing with Collin had thrown me for a loop.

I looked at the clock. It wasn't time for a break.

"I have time for a couple of questions."

A man raised his hand.

"What do you think about the rule, show don't tell?"

"Remember rule number one. There are no rules."

Everyone laughed.

"Seriously, that's a good question. I'm sick of hearing that phrase to be honest. Because you *tell* a story. You don't show a story. What I really think it means is that you don't want the reader to be disconnected from your character. You want them to feel what your character feels. To go through what they are going through. So to speak. You can't do that if you are simply describing the story. Does that make sense?"

"Not really," the man said.

What is it with men?

"For instance, let's say your character has a fight with her love interest. A trope that's present in almost every romance novel."

Why did I have to use that example? It didn't apply. Collin and I had a fight, but he wasn't my love interest.

"You could write the words, Josephine stormed off. That would be an example of describing the scene."

Like you did last night. Stormed off like a petulant child.

Shut up!

"Or you could say, Josephine stormed off so Col ... Cal wouldn't see her crying. The ache in her heart kept her up the entire night."

Like it did you.

He didn't break my heart. I was just mad.

"Adding those words makes a big difference for the readers," I explained. "You only added a few words, but now the reader is moved. You want them to feel what Josephine felt when she stormed off. She's afraid of being vulnerable. She doesn't want him to see the pain he has caused her."

My own words were condemning me.

Which is why you are emotionally unavailable to everyone else, I heard Collin say to me in my head.

His words echoed in my ears. Piercing me to the very core of my being.

Collin was right. Writing was a way for me to channel my pain and express it through my characters. So I didn't have to deal with the pain in real life. That's why I ran last night.

I owed Collin an apology.

After nearly thirty minutes of questions, the session ended, and I walked into the hallway and looked around. Hoping Collin was there. He wasn't.

I walked slowly to the elevators and went back to my room. Totally disgusted with myself and how I had behaved the night before and how poorly I had taught the class.

When I got to my room, I plopped down on the bed. Time for more introspection.

God told me to accept the invitation to dinner.

Now I knew why. And I blew it.

I was still emotionally stuck in May of 2023. Collin confronted me on it, and I lashed out at him for telling me the truth. I wished I could go back and tell him that.

It's too late.

***

Later that night

The last session of the writer's convention was an award's gala. My responsibilities were over, and I was able to sit back and relax, enjoy the dinner, and watch the faces of the finalists as the best book awards in various genres were announced.

I'd finally made peace with Collin in my mind, even though he was a thousand miles away and I'd never see him again. I understood now why God wanted me to go to dinner with him. To learn a valuable lesson.

I had isolated myself from everyone. Not just men.

When Mark died, my real life came to a halt. My fictional life as a writer exploded. My characters traveled all over the world. Experienced falling in love over and over again. Got married. Had children. Every book had a happy ending. That was demanded by romance readers.

Each time something exciting happened to one of my characters, I felt the joy. When they faced tragedy, I felt their pain. When they experienced their first kiss with a new love interest, my whole body tingled.

I did live vicariously through them. I got to experience those things over and over again, without the risk.

I didn't realize I was missing it in my own life. When I got back to San Diego, I intended to make some changes.

It didn't mean I was going to go seeking out men just to fall in love. But maybe I would write 5,000 words a day instead of ten. Or even 2,000 a day. Perhaps take more days off and not write any.

Nobody was making me write. I had no deadlines to meet. It was time for me to start living a life outside of my books.

The whole night was a blur. When the gala was over, I was swamped with attention. That prevented me from leaving right away. What I really wanted to do was get out of my formal dress. Go to bed and get up in the morning, eat breakfast, and catch my flight back to California.

I couldn't go back to my room. Dozens of women wanted to talk to me. I had books to sign. Pictures to pose for. Stories to hear. Questions to answer about their books.

I stayed and responded to every single person until no one was left. It's the least I could do, and I enjoyed every second of it.

My heart was content. The event in St. Louis had been a turning point for me. A divine encounter. I sensed my life was about to change.

While Mark would always be my first love, I was excited about the possibility of loving again. Having someone to share life with. Risking loss again. With Mark I hadn't even thought of the possibility of losing him. Not until we were old.

Now I knew it was a possibility at any stage in life. If God brought me someone new, I think I'd appreciate every day more. Knowing that it could end in a moment's notice.

"Thank you for everything, Jill," I said, as we prepared to leave. She seemed frazzled from running the event.

"Thank you. I'm so glad you came. You were wonderful. Everyone loves you."

She gave me a warm and sincere hug.

"I'm always so excited when the conference starts and so glad when it ends," Jill said.

"I know what you mean."

I looked up.

As if I sensed it.

Standing at the back in the doorway was Collin.

16

My heart leapt when I saw Collin standing in the doorway at the back of the grand ballroom. I could barely believe it. How was it possible? I was certain he had left my life forever.

I smiled. He waved sheepishly.

"Excuse me, Jill," I said. "I have to go."

The conference was over, and everyone had left the room except for Jill and a few of her staff.

After one more hug, she said. "We'll be in touch. Have a safe trip home."

I walked slowly toward the doorway where Collin was standing. He looked up at me, then down at his feet. Then back at me. Like he was extremely uncomfortable.

I wasn't the least bit nervous. For whatever reason, I felt an overwhelming peace.

"I'm happy to see your face," I said warmly, as I approached. Stopping a proper distance away, but close enough to reach out and touch him if he extended a hand.

His eyes widened like that wasn't the reaction he was expecting.

"I figured you never wanted to see me again."

"That's not true. I wanted to apologize. I felt bad about the way things ended last night."

He waved his hand dismissively.

"I'm the one who should apologize. I was totally out of line. I don't know what came over me."

"I know what came over you."

"You do? Well tell me."

"The same thing that came over me. We were both starting to open up to each other. For the first time since our spouses died. When it got too uncomfortable, you pushed me away. When it got too uncomfortable for me, I ran away, rather than confront my feelings."

"Are you the psychiatrist now?" He flashed a silly grin, so I'd know he was kidding.

I laughed to let him know I took it as a joke.

"I'm not a psychiatrist, but I did play one in one of my books," I quipped.

"I really am sorry," he said, with an achiness behind the words.

That was enough groveling from both of us. I decided to lighten the mood.

"It's forgiven. Hey, I thought you were going home today," I said.

"I did."

"You flew to Denver?"

His face flushed, like he was embarrassed. He still wouldn't look me in the eye and was fidgeting like a schoolboy talking to a pretty girl for the first time.

"I caught my flight this morning. When I landed in Denver, I caught the first flight back to St. Louis. Kind of stupid, huh?"

"You flew all the way back just to see me?"

He shrugged his shoulders.

"I couldn't leave things the way they were," he said. "I was totally out of line at dinner. That's not who I am. I'm really a nice guy when you get to know me."

"Obviously you're a nice guy, if you'd take all that time and spend all that money to come back just to apologize."

"It was the right thing to do. You deserved better than that."

Jill walked by and touched my arm. I blew her a kiss as she disappeared out the door.

"The thing about it is, you were right, Collin, when you said I use my books as a way to avoid getting close to other people. Especially men."

He winced.

"Did I really say that?"

I nodded.

"I'm sorry."

"You already said you were sorry. You don't have to say it again."

"I'm sorry." He put his hand over his mouth and laughed.

"Could we start over?" he asked.

"I'd like that."

He held out his hand.

"Hi. My name is Collin."

I shook it. "My name is Mia. Just so you know, I'm not emotionally unavailable anymore. Try me. Ask me a question."

That cracked us both up. I felt the tension releasing in him. I was so relaxed and not nervous that I was beginning to wonder what was wrong with me. It's like the peace that surpasses all understanding had taken over my body.

I certainly didn't understand it. Last night, I was shaking like a leaf on the inside. As uncomfortable as a turtle on a freeway. That's probably why I went into my shell at the first opportunity.

"Opposites do attract," Collin said. "You might be emotionally available, but I'm an emotional basket case."

The first flash of anxiety rose up inside of me.

Was I attracted to him?

I think so.

"Would you like to have dinner with me?" he asked.

Was he attracted to me?

Duh.

I grimaced on the inside. A big part of me wanted a do-over from last night. Dinner would be a good opportunity to reset things. I looked back at the banquet hall. The staff was busy tearing down all the tables where the thousand plus people had just consumed a meal of stuffed chicken, salad, russet potatoes, veggies, bread, and dessert.

My lips twisted to the side. "I already ate. I'm sorry. Otherwise, I would love to."

I rubbed my stomach.

"About two hours ago, this tight-fitting dress actually fit me," I said. "That's before I ate a big meal. Now it's way too tight. I'm sorry. Raincheck?"

That sounded like a stupid thing to say. When would we get the opportunity for a raincheck? He lived in Denver. My flight left early in the morning. After tonight, I literally would never see him again.

"Oh. Well okay."

He looked around. The banquet hall was about empty. We stepped outside into the hallway and an employee closed the door behind us. The vendor booths were gone. We were the only two people left in the area.

"I've obviously taken enough of your time," he said. "I'm really glad I caught you and we had this chance to talk. I wish you all the best."

Was that it?

He flew all the way back from Denver to apologize to me and I rejected him a second time.

I don't want dinner. I'm full. The voice in my head said the words in a mocking tone.

Was I that cruel? I felt bad. I also didn't want the conversation to end.

"Can you meet me in the lobby in ten minutes?" I blurted out before giving myself a chance to think about it.

"Sure."

"I need to go to my room and get out of this dress. But I'll meet you in the lobby."

"Sounds good."

"Are you hungry?" I asked.

"Not really. I ate on the plane."

I glanced out the window. From our vantage point, I could see the arch.

"Do you want to take a walk? It looks like the sun is starting to set. I bet it's pretty out by the Mississippi River and the arch."

"That sounds great. I'll see you in ten minutes."

Then we realized at the same time that we both had to go to the elevators to get to our rooms. He motioned in that direction and we walked together to the elevators. He pushed the up button. When it arrived, and we stepped in, he asked me what floor.

"Nine, please."

Even though he pushed the nine button, it didn't light up and the elevator didn't move even though the door was closed.

"It requires a room key," I said.

"Oh right. I forgot."

He produced one out of his pocket, touched his key to the sensor, and pushed nine which lit up. He pushed the top floor button where he must be staying.

The penthouse maybe. I really didn't know much about him other than that he sold some kind of commercial product. He must be doing well if he could afford a room on the top floor.

I didn't say anything.

By the time I got back to my room, my heart was fluttering with anticipation. It was nothing like getting ready for my first date with Mark. We were a couple of college kids who decided to hang out one night with some friends. Every other date after the first one was pretty much the same. Neither of us had any money, so we mostly entertained ourselves with stuff we could do for free. Food we could eat for cheap.

This felt like a real date, and I prepped like it was.

I peeled off the dress and used everything in the bathroom I had at my disposal to make me feel and smell like a woman. After using half of my ten minutes, I inspected myself in the mirror. I didn't look bad since I had spent more than an hour and a half getting ready for the ball not that long ago.

My hair looked good. I brushed my teeth and refreshed my deodorant. Sprayed a slight mist of perfume on my neck, then rubbed some on my wrists.

As I rummaged through my luggage for something to wear, I couldn't help but wonder what had brought Collin all the way back to St. Louis. I told him it didn't seem weird, but in retrospect, it did. That's a lot of effort to go through for a woman you just met.

An expensive apology.

Was it only to apologize? Did he have something else in mind?

For whatever reason, I wasn't leery.

I even told him what floor my room was on. I hadn't felt the need to use any precautions. I didn't even mind being alone with him by the arch. Surely, God would warn me if something was amiss.

It didn't seem like he came back hoping to take advantage of me in some way. It seemed like he was genuinely sorry about what happened. It was a touching gesture. I doubted few men alive would go to that effort without expecting something in return.

As soon as I found a comfortable pair of jeans and a light sleeveless shirt and sweater, I headed down to the lobby to meet him. He was waiting for me, looking handsome in his button-up shirt and khakis. The first time I'd seen him without a jacket.

"Ready to go?" he asked, holding out his arm.

I took it, feeling a flutter in my stomach. This was definitely a date. And I was definitely attracted to him.

As we walked through the hotel lobby and exited the hotel, Collin filled me in on his flight back from Denver. He told me about the turbulence, the crying baby, and the elderly couple sitting across from him.

"The only thing good about the flight back was the meal."

That surprised me. I'd had airplane food a number of times.

"What did you have?"

"I had the filet. With salad and potatoes."

"So you were in first class?"

"Yes. I always fly first when I can. Once you fly first, it's hard to go back."

That's one luxury I allowed myself when I flew. I wanted to ask how much the ticket was but didn't dare. He obviously could afford it.

"Did you shower?" I asked.

"I did."

"How on earth did you have time to shower in ten minutes?"

"I don't know. I'm fast I guess."

I could smell the mixture of shampoo, soap, shaving cream, and aftershave on him.

"Men are so lucky," I said. "It'd take me an hour to do all of that."

"That's because you're already beautiful."

"Flattery will get you everywhere, kind sir," I said, while squeezing his arm tighter.

He pointed to his face with his free hand.

"I had to take a shower. I felt grungy from spending the entire day on the plane. But, anything longer than ten minutes would be a waste of time. This is the best I can do. Even if I spent an hour, it wouldn't get any better than this."

"You look fabulous, darling," I said in an accent mimicking a famous line from a television show.

To get to the arch, all we had to do was walk outside the hotel and turn left and we were in its monstrous shadow. The sun was setting to the west, behind us, and cast a fiery glow on the top of the silver arch whose graceful curve reached toward the heavens. It was a breathtaking sight to behold.

We stopped to admire it.

"Did you know you can go up the arch?" I said.

"I did know that. I never have. Do you want to?"

"It looks like it's closed," I said.

"That's all right. I'm enjoying the view from here."

"This path leads to the river."

We set out walking again. A few people were out on the paved walkway. Several runners. A couple of bikers caught Collin's eye. A couple was passionately kissing on one of the benches which caused me to blush.

Fortunately, Collin was looking at a biker and didn't notice my red cheeks.

We came to the other side of the arch and stopped at the overlook and leaned against the railing. The shimmering shadow of the huge monument reflected on the Mississippi River. I moaned my approval.

The sun had transformed the sky into a canvas of orange and red hues. The water below rippled gently, the reflection of the arch danced on the surface.

"This is incredible," I said barely above a whisper, feeling a sense of calm wash over me.

"It is," Collin agreed, keeping his eyes fixed on the river and its magnificent view.

We stood there in silence for a few moments, taking it all in.

"It's so beautiful," I said.

"Yes, you are," he said.

I didn't know when it happened. Suddenly we were comfortable with each other. I leaned my head on his shoulder.

"Do you want to walk?" he asked.

"No. I want to stay like this," I said, sweetly.

It felt good. I felt protected. Had I been alone, I would've been petrified. A single woman walking alone by the river in downtown St. Louis at dusk, would be foolish.

Collin was taller than I thought. His shoulders broader. I could feel his biceps through his thin sleeve. He obviously did work out.

The evening was warm, and I didn't need my sweater, so I took it off and wrapped it around my waist. Collin put his arm on my bare shoulder and pulled me closer. I could feel the heat radiating off his body and it was strangely comforting.

"You know, you're really beautiful," he said, his voice low and husky. "I wasn't just saying that."

I blushed, feeling a sense of warmth spread through my body. It had been a long time since I had been complimented in that way.

"Thank you," I said softly.

In unison, we turned and faced each other. I looked up and into his eyes.

He leaned in and confidently and without hesitation brushed my lips with his own. It was a gentle kiss, lasting only a few seconds, but there was an intensity to it that made my knees weak.

It was like nothing else mattered in the world.

When we finally slowly moved our heads away from each other, Collin grinned at me, his eyes sparkling with a mischievous glint. With his left hand, he reached over and pushed a lock of hair off my face and gently brushed it behind my ear. Sending a chill down my spine.

"Thank you for coming back for me," I said, in a tone that matched the softness of the mood.

"You're welcome. I'm glad I did."

"Last night, when I envisioned seeing you again, in my wildest dreams, I never imagined I'd be standing by the arch, letting you kiss me."

"I wanted to see you again. When I saw you in the ballroom, I was afraid that you hated me."

My breath caught in my throat. I wet my lips with my tongue. Instinctively.

My heart began to race. I leaned in this time. Our lips met in a deeper, more passionate kiss that was as short as the first one, but more intense as I pressed my lips into his.

All of the emotions began to flood my soul at once.

"There. Do you know now that I don't hate you?"

Collin's arms folded around me, and I collapsed onto his chest.

And cried.

He held me tighter.

I found something inside of me that I thought died with Mark.

It was like Collin knew exactly what I needed at that moment. He didn't say anything, just held me until the tears faded away.

I'd been holding onto my pain for too long.

Collin had given me permission to let it go.

God told me now was the time.

Three months later, we were engaged. Nine months later we were married.

17

Five years later

The New Horizons II spacecraft had been in the Kuiper Belt for more than three months. Running tests and sending data back to NASA in real time. The results were finally in.

A group of high-level scientists poured over the data and met to discuss the findings. A report was prepared. The director of NASA, Dr. Lesley Ramsey, was called to present the findings to the president and his cabinet.

Ramsey walked into the west wing of the White House for only the second time in his distinguished career. The first time was when he had been sworn into his position. He didn't place his hand on the Bible as most of his predecessors had done. He placed it on Tristam Brand's book called, *The Colorful Insignificant Dot*.

Written more than five decades ago, the book was the bible in astronomy circles as far as Ramsey was concerned. The title came from a picture taken of earth from a probe many years before. Earth was nothing but a small blue dot. Hence the title.

Ramsey's other idol, Bertrand Russell, once wrote, "nobody can prove that there is not between Earth and Mars a China teapot revolving in an elliptical orbit, but nobody thinks this sufficiently likely to be taken into account in practice. I think the Christian god just as unlikely."

After the first New Horizons probe, Ramsey wrote his own article for publication. The basic premise being that the expedition did indeed prove that there was no teapot between Earth and Mars, Chinese or otherwise. It also proved with reasonable certainty that there was no god as well.

Surely, if god existed, they would've seen some evidence of him somewhere in the universe. Ramsey explained in the paper that he started his career as an agnostic, but turned into what he called an atheistic scientist. Whenever he conducted an experiment, he assumed there was no god to interfere, since he never had.

His work in the New Horizons probe and his academically acclaimed paper propelled him rapidly up the ladder at NASA until he ascended to the top of the food chain and was appointed to be the director.

Many Christians in congress opposed his appointment, but the president supported his friend and his beliefs. They went to college together and had maintained that friendship through the years. Helping each other along the way.

President George Heath was an atheist as well but a practicing Christian for political expediency. Ramsey couldn't keep the subterfuge himself but admired his friend's ability to perform for an audience. The president dutifully bowed his head during prayers. Regularly attended church. Placed his hand on the Bible when taking the oath of office. He even told the country to pray for the nation and victims in tragedies. He even used the term, God Bless America at the end of each speech.

Ramsey couldn't wait to present his findings. Rarely, if ever, did the director of NASA get an audience with the president. He was led through the metal detectors by a staffer and taken to the Cabinet Room in the west wing. Just off the Oval Office and the president's private office.

He would have thirty minutes to present his findings. He presumed the meeting would go longer based on the bombshell information he was bringing them.

Everyone but the president was in the room waiting. After the introductions, Ramsey was asked to take a seat at the far end of the massive conference table, opposite the president. The findings sat in front of him in bound folders ready to present to the already bored-looking participants.

They won't be bored for long, he mused to himself.

The president entered and Ramsey didn't stand since none of the other cabinet members did either. President Heath caught his friend's eye and motioned for him to begin.

Ramsey stood to his feet.

"The New Horizons II is part of our New Frontiers program," he said, shaking out the frog in his throat with the first words. "Part of my mission as director has been to find new points of exploration that will give us the most information and results based on the budget."

"Spending money wisely is always a good thing," the president said.

Ramsey nodded.

"New Horizons II was sent to the Kuiper Belt. In search of evidence of intelligent life, based on a theory propagated by Dr. Mark Cooper, of the University of California, San Diego department of science. Dr. Cooper has since deceased."

Several nodded as if they knew that and probably knew the circumstances of his death.

Ramsey hadn't been impressed by Cooper's report. It had an inane reference to God in one of the footnotes. It attributed the formation of the heart of Pluto to a higher power even though there was no evidence to back up his theory.

The evidence was already conclusive. The heart was nothing more than frozen hydrogen ice in a basin probably formed millions of years ago when a meteor crashed into the side of the planet. If a god was behind it, he certainly lacked creativity and had limited abilities in Ramsey's mind.

Ramsey wouldn't have approved the mission, but his predecessor had done so, and he had inherited the probe. Now he was glad. The results were astonishing. He would go down in history as the man who oversaw it.

"New Horizons II stopped at Uranus first, then Neptune, and lastly Pluto. A smaller probe was sent from New Horizons into the atmosphere of each planet. As far as Uranus and Neptune, there's not really a surface to land on so to speak. These are gaseous planets. We call them ice giants. Which complicates entry. They consist of mostly fluids blown around by a swirling wind. We developed a drone that could withstand the elements long enough to send us the necessary data."

"What were the findings?" the president asked. A no-nonsense man who usually got right to the point.

"We discovered the presence of radioactive material in the atmosphere of both planets."

Ramsey saw their eyes widen. A few sat forward in their chairs. None were taking notes even though they all had pen and paper nearby.

"The probe continued on to Pluto where we sent another drone to land on the surface, in the heart shaped area. It took samples of the ice and sent back the results. A second drone landed on the surface outside of the heart and took samples of the soil and rock."

"For what purpose?"

"To determine if there was radioactive material on Pluto and also to determine if the debris in the Kuiper Belt came from Pluto."

"What would that prove?"

"That an explosion on Pluto caused the debris field in the Kuiper Belt. Dr. Mark Cooper's theory was that life once existed on Pluto.

He purported that a nuclear war caused the massive hole on the side of Pluto which filled up with ice causing the heart shape we see on pictures."

"Go on," the president said.

"New Horizons II continued traveling through the Kuiper Belt landing on various debris structures and taking samples. For the purpose of comparing those samples with the ones we took from each planet. We wanted to see if they matched. To see if we could conclusively prove that the debris in the Kuiper Belt came from one or more of the planets."

"And?" the president said. "Let's hear the punch line."

"We now have conclusive findings."

Ramsey gathered the reports in his hand. He passed them out to the various cabinet members.

"You will find the summary of the findings in paragraph one of the first page. I think it's self-explanatory."

The president's eyes widened when he read the first paragraph.

Several of the cabinet members' mouths gaped open.

The director of homeland security spoke up first, "I suggest that we classify this report and not release it to the public."

"Classify it?" the president asked.

"Yes. Give it the highest classification. We don't want this information in the hands of the public until we know what to do with it."

The president nodded slowly, his mind was obviously racing with the implications of the report.

Ramsey agreed. Had the director of homeland security not suggested it, he would've. This information needed to be handled with the utmost care.

"Does everyone agree?" the president asked.

They all nodded.

"Then it's done."

Ramsey was relieved.

***

San Diego

"Classified?" I had said to Dr. Cecilia Steele when she told me the news.

Two hours ago, she called to tell me she'd been notified by NASA that the results of the probe were going to be classified.

For fifty years!

I'd been expecting a call for weeks. Out of all the possible results, this was one I had never considered.

Waiting for Collin to get home to tell him had been excruciating. He was golfing with Cecilia's husband. After that first lunch with Cecilia years ago, we started making it a weekly thing. After Collin and I married, our husbands became fast friends as well.

We joined the same country club where I still had lunch with my girlfriends. While I didn't play golf, we were at the club a lot. The monthly membership required us to spend a minimum amount each month on food in the restaurant.

Between lunches with Cecilia and my girlfriends, Collin's golf outings, and our Friday night card games, we usually ate more than the allowance and owed money at the end of each month.

Collin finally arrived home, pleased with his golf play that day. Which wasn't always the case. I hated to ruin it for him by sharing my distressing news.

He was barely through the door when I ran up to him and blurted, "Cecilia heard from NASA."

"Lucas told me," Collin said. "Cecilia called him while we were golfing."

"So you know that NASA has classified the results from Mark's probe?"

"I know."

"For fifty years!"

"It's unbelievable."

"How can they do that?"

He walked past me and into the kitchen after kissing me on the lips. Walked over to the fridge and took out a cold soft drink. Popped the cap and took a big swig. We both leaned against the kitchen island.

"They are the government," he said, with a hint of bitterness behind the tone. "They can do whatever they want."

"I thought they were going to say that Mark was wrong. That the tests proved there never was life on Pluto."

"I think this proves that Mark was right. They did discover proof of life on Pluto, and they're covering it up."

Collin had been extremely protective of Mark and his legacy. I still had a picture of Mark and me on the wall in the den. He had a picture of his wife Martha with his daughter Sandy next to it. A portrait of us together hung above the fireplace.

I appreciated that he didn't mind talking about Mark with me, and I didn't mind him talking about Martha. We both had a life before we got married. Our spouses meant a lot to us at the time. Still did. That didn't mean we loved each other less.

It made things easier for me that he had never had the slightest hint of jealousy or tried to ask me to compare them. Good thing because we had talked about the probe a lot over the last five years.

"Cecilia said she thinks it goes to the highest levels of our government," I said. "All the way to the president himself."

"Wouldn't surprise me one bit. Did you know that more than two billion documents have been classified by our government? That's ridiculous."

Collin was a bit of a conspiracy theorist. Extremely untrusting of our government. I never went as far as he did. I was beginning to wonder if he was right now that I was seeing it firsthand. I couldn't think of one logical reason why the public shouldn't know the results of those findings.

"Why can't they tell us the results?" I whined. "At least tell Cecilia. She has a security clearance. They said the results are highly classified. Above her level of clearance."

"Look at the Kennedy assassination," he said. "It's been more than eighty years, and they still haven't released the classified documents. The family can't even get them."

"Why though? What are they trying to hide?"

"It's not just that. It's elitism. They think we can't handle the truth."

"We have a right to know. The American people paid for that expedition. It was Mark's idea for heaven's sake!"

"That's not how they look at it. They are the elites. We are the peons. They tell us what they think we need to know."

"They're treating us like children."

"I don't disagree."

I collapsed into his arms. He wrapped his big arms around me and squeezed. I couldn't help but cry. I was so disappointed. I'd been waiting five years for this. Ever since I learned that NASA approved the probe, I had such high hopes. That Mark would be proven right.

Collin leaned in closer, his voice dropping to a whisper. "We can't just sit here and do nothing, Mia. We have to do something."

"I know," I said. "But what can we do?"

Collin's voice became excited. He released me and stepped back a couple of paces.

"If they discovered life on Pluto, it could change everything we know about the universe. I think it proves the existence of God as well. Not that it should've ever been in doubt. But how would they argue evolution on two different planets at the same time? With the same DNA!"

"Do you think that's why they're covering it up? Because they discovered human DNA on Pluto?"

"That's the only thing that makes sense. Why else would they try to bury the information?"

"What can we do about it?"

"We can leak it to the press. Anonymously. Get the word out before the government can silence us."

"They'll know we did it."

"But what can they do to us?"

"I don't know. Cecilia warned me not to say a word to anyone. That we could get in a lot of trouble."

"I don't care. Do you?"

"Not really. I think the truth should come out."

"I agree."

My cell phone rang about that time. It was sitting on the kitchen counter. Collin was closest and answered it.

"This is her husband," he said.

"Who is it?" I asked.

He didn't answer. Also didn't really say anything for the entire conversation so I couldn't tell who was on the other end of the call. Based on his furrowed brow, it was something important. He hung up the mysterious phone call about a minute later.

"That was someone with the president's office," he said soberly.

"The university?"

"No. The President of the United States. He was with the legal counsel to the president. He basically said that we could not disclose anything regarding the probe, Mark's paper, the results, anything for a period of fifty years."

"I'll be ninety-one-years-old. I don't know if I'll live that long."

***

I almost did live that long.

I made it to ninety. Three weeks shy of my ninety-first birthday.

My life had been wonderful. Collin passed away seven years before me. I was so lucky to fall in love twice. Both times with such amazing men.

Collin and I built a great life together. When we first met, he told me he was a refrigeration salesman. Turns out, he owned the company. Eventually, he sold the company for seven hundred million dollars and moved to San Diego.

Ironically enough, our relationship with the University of California San Diego was one of the highlights of my life. Since Cecilia and I were best friends, it opened all sorts of doors. Including speaking one year at the graduation ceremonies.

Cecilia retired about ten years ago and died three months later. It's like her whole life was given to running that department at the university. Once she didn't have that, she lost the will to live.

When I die, a fairly substantial endowment will go to the Mark Cooper science department. To renovate his building.

I had a strong motivation to keep living. I had to know what was in that classified document. In nine months, the results were supposed to be declassified.

We had tried to get the information declassified over the years. Even considered going to the press several times, but we were threatened with criminal prosecution if we revealed any of the details.

So, I fought as long as I could to make it the fifty years.

But my body was failing.

Fortunately, I was able to remain at home in my last days. A full-time live-in nurse took care of me. I barely weighed a hundred pounds with my shoes and clothes on.

I wrote novels until the strain on my eyes wouldn't let me do it anymore. More than 400 books. After book 200, I did it more for pleasure than anything else. I began to write romance novels set on other planets beside Pluto.

It seemed like today was the day when I'd finally leave the earth.

The nurse had said as much. She urged me to go to the hospital, but I insisted on staying home. Also, refused heavy medication. I wanted my senses about me when I said my goodbyes.

The nurse called Sandy, Collin's daughter. She lived nearby. She's been like the daughter I never had. I filled the void for the mom she lost. To the best I could.

Sandy married a fantastic man who Collin and I loved, and they had two marvelous daughters. My granddaughters, Emma and Rose. I treated them like my own flesh and blood, and they didn't know the difference. Sandy's husband's mom died when he was a teenager, so I was the only grandmother they'd ever known.

They called me Nana and my heart warmed every time I heard the name. They're the only reason I kept the big house after Collin died. It had a pool and they loved spending time with me. Listening to my stories. Reading my books when they were old enough.

We set up trust funds for them. They'd both get a fairly substantial sum of money when I passed.

They were both there in my room. Their eyes were heavy with grief and love. I wanted to take away their pain and stay longer, but I was ready to go on and be with Jesus. To be with Mark and Collin.

I drifted in and out of consciousness. My eyes would close, and I would fade into a peaceful rest. Each time Emma would clutch my hand and shake it slightly. Like she wanted to make sure I was still alive.

Rose was on the other side of my bed grasping my other hand. Both were emotional, but she was the stronger of the two.

"It's okay, Nana. You can go if you need to," she whispered in my ear. "You can go be with Papa."

Their name for Collin.

"I don't want you to go," Emma said, her voice trembling. "We love you so much, Nana,"

"We'll miss you," Rose said. "But we know it's time."

I didn't really have the strength to answer, but I managed a faint smile.

"Do you see him?" I said, when a sudden strength came over me.

"See who, Nana?" Rose asked.

I was able to raise my hand and point in the air.

"Over there. Do you see Jesus? He's coming for me."

"I don't see anything," Emma said.

"Go ahead and go with him," Rose said. "We'll be okay."

My eyes were fixed on the radiant figure. As my breathing grew slower, my senses increased. I could see him more clearly. The brightness around him should've been blinding but it invigorated my soul.

I heard Sandy's voice. I could tell she had entered the room even though my eyes were closed.

How could I see Jesus with my eyes closed?

"Is Nana dead?" Emma asked, through the tears.

Sandy put her fingers on the side of my neck to check for a pulse.

"Not yet. Soon dear."

She touched my shoulder and leaned over and kissed my forehead.

"I love you. Thank you for being so wonderful to daddy and to me and the girls."

"Thank you for being the best grandmother ever!" Emma said.

I opened my eyes one last time. Sandy's eyes were peaceful and filled with love.

"We'll miss you," she said.

I felt a smile come on my lips.

Then I took one last shallow breath and closed my eyes for the last time.

Except I didn't see darkness. I didn't see the figure of Jesus either, but I felt his presence. A brilliant light was drawing me toward him.

My entire life had led me to this moment. I'd written hundreds of books about love and romance. I was suddenly immersed in love. Like I'd never experienced before.

I reached out toward the light and felt an ocean of peace wash over me.

As I drew closer to the light, I began to hear whispers. At first, they were faint. They grew louder. They were the voices of all the people I had loved and lost over the years. My parents. Mark. Collin. Cecilia. Her husband. They were all there. Welcoming me. Standing behind Jesus.

I fell at his feet and worshiped him.

He lifted my head so my eyes could gaze on him.

I suddenly had a new body. A spiritual body. No more pain. No more sorrow.

Within seconds, maybe minutes, maybe instantly, I knew exactly what had happened on Pluto and what was in that classified document.

18

Nine months later

Newly elected president, Joe Bob Belken, was a good old southern boy from Alabama. A fundamentally conservative governor who ran on an America First agenda and won forty-nine states. Even winning the liberal state of California.

The only thing he hated worse than big government, was LSU football. A big rival of his favorite team, the Alabama Crimson Tide. He ran on the slogan Drain The Bayou. An obvious reference to the nearby state of Louisiana, which he managed to carry by thirty points, even with the obvious dig in his campaign rhetoric.

One of his basic tenets was to shrink the "bloated" government. Along those lines he was in the process of slashing budgets and laying off government employees. To fulfill one of the promises he made on the campaign trail, he was going through and declassifying millions of documents.

Things such as the names of CIA operatives, war plans, covert operations, etc., should be classified in his mind. The public had a right to know almost everything else.

Declassification was the agenda again that morning. His chief of staff, Eddie Brewer sat in the president's private office with a pile of papers stacked on the round conference table and a list of documents to consider.

Several members of the president's cabinet had protested. Saying they should be in on the decisions. A heated discussion had broken out at the last cabinet meeting.

"The American people voted me president," Joe said vehemently. "Not you. You serve at my whim. I'm perfectly capable of deciding what should and shouldn't be classified."

The power did lie with him. He could declassify anything he wanted, and no one could stop him. As he sat in his chair at the conference table reviewing the documents one by one, he couldn't help but feel a rush of excitement. The thought of revealing secrets that had been hidden for years gave him a sense of power that he had never experienced before.

Things were moving along quickly. So far, he hadn't deemed anything worthy of security clearance. He picked up the next document on the list and read through it quickly. It was a report on a covert operation in the Middle East that had taken place during the previous administration. Joe had always been critical of the previous president's foreign policy, and he relished the opportunity to expose any wrongdoing.

With a flick of his wrist, Joe stamped "Declassified" on the document and tossed it onto the pile of papers that had already been reviewed. He continued on, methodically going through each report, and deeming them fit for public consumption.

After they'd worked through almost everything in the stack, Eddie handed him another classified document.

"I saved the best two for last," he said. "This has been classified for fifty years. It's set to expire this month."

"As a general rule, I don't think anything should be classified longer than ten years. Unless it really is a threat to national security."

"Agreed. This is a NASA document."

"Why would anything in outer space ever be classified?"

"You'll see."

"Did we discover aliens on another planet?" he quipped.

"Something like that."

The president was surprised by Eddie's response. He had been joking and Eddie's tone didn't match his own.

He flipped over the folder and read the first paragraph to himself.

The New Horizons II probe discovered definitive proof of life on other planets.

Another jolt of excitement ripped through him. Many Americans for decades had believed the government had been hiding the existence of intelligent life in the universe. The zealots had turned the idea of UFO's, alien invaders, and Area 51, into a commercial enterprise.

The report was more than a hundred pages. He flipped to the end. To his surprise, he didn't see any mention of anything that might confirm the far fetched ideas purported by the conspiracy theorists. The details must be buried in the report.

"Give me the cliff notes version," the president said.

"The New Horizons II probe was sent to the outer planets, Neptune and Uranus, and also Pluto. Based on a theory developed by a Christian scientist, Dr. Mark Cooper, from the University of California, San Diego. He believed in the existence of God."

"I like him already."

"On the side of Pluto is a heart."

The president had seen the picture on page three of the classified report.

"I didn't know that. But I barely passed science in school," he said.

"You don't have to be a science major to understand what I'm about to tell you."

"I'm listening."

"Dr. Cooper's theory was that Pluto sustained life at some point. He believed that the people on Pluto engaged in a nuclear war and blew up the side of their own planet. That's what formed the heart."

"I'm shocked we haven't done the same thing here on earth."

Eddie nodded.

"That's part of the purpose of the probe. In Dr. Cooper's mind, if he could prove that the people of Pluto destroyed themselves with nuclear weapons, it might help us think twice before doing the same."

"Smart man."

"He also thought it might prove the existence of God. If there was once life on Pluto, with the same DNA as earthlings, it would blow the whole idea of evolution out of the water and disprove it once and for all."

"It's already disproved as far as I'm concerned. The whole idea that we evolved from apes is ludicrous."

"Turns out Dr. Cooper was wrong about Pluto but on the right track."

"How so?"

"The probe took samples from Neptune and Uranus. It discovered the presence of radioactive material. Similar to nuclear fallout when we explode a nuclear bomb on earth."

"That's interesting."

"It gets better."

"I can't wait to hear it."

"Samples were taken from various pieces of floating debris in the Kuiper Belt. Which is the vast expanse around the planets. The area is filled with rock and ice formations. From those samples, scientists were able to determine that the pieces came not just from Pluto, but from Uranus and Neptune as well."

"So a massive explosion on those planets was what likely sent the debris into space? Possibly by a nuke?"

"Probably a nuke. Since they found traces of radioactive material in the pieces of rocks in the Kuiper Belt from all three planets."

"Interesting. But I still don't see why this information was classified."

"They also found human DNA on the rocks from Neptune and Uranus. Consistent with humans on earth."

The president sat forward in his chair.

"So this Dr. Cooper was right?"

"Partially. They didn't find any human DNA from the rocks that originated from Pluto."

The president rubbed his eyes roughly.

"I'm not sure I'm following."

"It means all three planets were affected by the nuclear explosions. But Neptune and Uranus once sustained human life. Pluto didn't."

"Not necessarily. All that proves is that no humans were caught up in the nuclear explosion on Pluto. That doesn't mean they didn't exist. Any chance the people on Pluto were the ones who blew Neptune and Uranus to smithereens?"

"Anything is possible."

"I still don't know why the American people couldn't have this information."

"There's more. I must warn you that the information is deeply disturbing."

"Okay."

The president's heart whipped around in anticipation.

"When the probe landed on Pluto, it picked up sounds."

"What kind of sounds?"

"Voices."

"People?"

"Correct. People speaking English."

"Are you telling me there are Americans on Pluto right now?"

"And Germans. And Russians. And Mexicans. The probe picked up thousands of discernible voices. Speaking various languages."

"How is that possible?"

"We don't know."

"What were they saying?"

"It appeared that the people were in distress. It picked up crying. Moaning. Shouting. Cries for help."

The president couldn't believe what he was hearing.

"I'm skeptical. Are they really sure the voices were real?"

"They recorded them. I've heard some of them. They are chilling."

"What have we done about it?"

"After we discovered the information, we sent two more probes to Pluto. With better equipment."

"And?"

"Both probes found the same thing. Only with more certainty. It seemed like thousands of people, maybe millions are trapped in the core of Pluto. Crying out for help."

"Why didn't we organize a rescue mission?"

"There's no telling how thick the ice is. We don't know how we can get to them."

"I agree that this should remain classified. For ten more years. I want NASA to get to work on a rescue mission to Pluto."

"Done."

The president slumped back in his chair, trying to consider all the ramifications of this new information.

"What else you got?" he asked.

"The Kennedy assassination. November 22, 1963."

The president's heart skipped another beat. He used the Kennedy classification of documents on the campaign trail as an example of the ridiculousness of the United States government. Keeping this information classified for more than a hundred and twenty-one years was beyond ridiculous.

"I've been wanting to see this one," the president said. "Why in the world has this been classified for so long?"

Eddie pulled out a folder and handed it to the president, who opened it and read the contents of the first page. A summary of findings.

"See for yourself," Eddie said.

President Joe Bob Belken looked it over for nearly three minutes.

He slammed the folder shut.

"Keep it classified. For fifty more years!"

19

In heaven, all mysteries of the universe are revealed to you immediately. Although the things of earth and past life aren't as important anymore.

Between spending time with my loved ones and worshiping Jesus, there wasn't much time to concern myself with questions that perplexed me on earth. In fact, there wasn't any time at all since it didn't exist in heaven.

I thought I'd tell you what happened though. So you'd know.

Maybe it'd help you somehow in your own life on earth. I was a storyteller in my life, so I thought I'd tell you the story of what happened to the people on two planets nearly two billion miles from our own.

Each planet of the solar system once contained life. Along with a garden of Eden, an Adam and an Eve, and a tree of the knowledge of good and evil. All the planets eventually ate of the tree bringing sin into the world.

The planet Neptune had one language, and everyone spoke the same words. They all migrated to the east and settled together. One man, Xion, feared God and shunned evil. Another man, Bale, did more evil in the sight of the Lord than any of those before him.

Against Xion's wishes, Bale encouraged the people to build a tower to the heavens.

"Come and help me build," he implored the people. "So that we can make a name for ourselves."

"No!" Xion said. "This will be an abomination to the Lord."

One third of the people supported Xion. Two thirds helped build the city and the tower.

When the Lord saw it, he was displeased. He confused their language and drove the followers of Bale to the planet we called Uranus. During that time, the two planets were connected by a ring. The people walked across and settled on the new planet.

Once across, the Lord destroyed the ring and separated Neptune from Uranus and made the people of Neptune his chosen people. He brought favor upon them.

The people in Uranus lived with constant hardship. For that reason, Bale hated Xion and the people of Neptune and vowed to kill them. Not unlike the wars between the Arabs and the Jews on earth.

All of the planets had the same types of problems. War and evil was part of man's sinful nature, that came from the fall.

Weapons were devised from nuclear reactions. The leaders of both planets built missiles in the form of arrows and launched them at each other, but none found their mark. Many of them landed on the side of Pluto. Creating large indentations on its side. Several eventually crashed through to its inner core.

Still, the wicked leaders persisted.

Until they eventually blew each other up and all that was left were the two gaseous planets that could no longer sustain life. The debris scattered through the Kuiper Belt. The New Horizons II probe discovered the truth.

It also found hell.

The nuclear weapons turned the core of Pluto into a fiery inferno. Part of God's eternal plan. God created hell for the devil and his demons.

It was God's desire that none perish but all have eternal life in heaven.

But the faithless, the ones who rejected Christ were cast into the lake of fire that burned with fire and sulfur. The second death.

When I arrived in heaven, my name was found in the Lambs Book of Life and I was allowed to enter into eternal life in heaven. Those who had rejected Christ were blotted out of the book and cast away into eternal punishment.

"You were right," I said to Mark when we had a chance to discuss it.

"I had to go all the way to heaven to finally hear those words from you," he joked.

We laughed. Our lives were so full of joy.

"The heart of Pluto was formed by God," I said.

"Yes it was, Mia. As a sign. Like the rainbow."

"God was saying to the universe that his heart is that none should perish but that all should have eternal life."

The End

FROM THE AUTHOR

I hope you have enjoyed *The Eden Stories* as much as I have enjoyed writing them. I also hope you take them in the spirit in which they were written. I've always had a strong belief in the inerrant word of God and the value it adds to our lives. I've taken many liberties in the books and created fictional accounts and characters that loosely mirror those in Scripture.

Not to in any way belittle, add to, or take away from the power of the Word of God, but with the sincere hope that the stories might cause the reader to go back and read the biblical accounts and learn from them.

So if anyone is offended by the effort, then I apologize. It's intended to be fiction. When God is speaking in one of the books, I tried my best to stay true to the God who never changes.

If these books have drawn you closer to God, then I have accomplished my main goal. If you've given your heart to Jesus through the gospel presentation in the words I penned, then even better.

I'd love to hear from you if you were saved through reading one of the books. Or if you just have something to say to me. I respond to all of my emails. Usually within a few days of receiving them. You can reach out to me at terry@terrytoler.com.

Thank you again for supporting my books and making them best sellers.

I love you all, dearly.

Terry Toler

Thank you for purchasing this novel from best-selling author, Terry Toler. As an additional thank you, Terry wants to give you a free gift.

Sign up for:

Updates
New Releases
Announcements

At terrytoler.com

We'll send you an eBook, *The Book Club*, a Cliff Hangers novella, free of charge.

READ MORE BOOKS FROM TERRY TOLER

Jamie Austen Thrillers

Read all the Jamie Austen Thrillers. They must be good.
They've been number one on Amazon in ten different countries.
Click on the link below.

THE JAMIE AUSTEN THRILLERS (12 book series)
Kindle Edition (amazon.com)

https://amzn.to/3vmPUy7

Cliff Hangers Mystery Series

Who wants to read a good mystery? We've got you covered! Read the Cliff Hangers where homicide detective, Cliff Ford, solves crimes in Chicago, with help from his wife Julia. These books have everything Terry Toler is known for. Page turning suspense, a hint of romance, and an ending you won't see coming.

The Cliff Hangers Mystery Series (4 book series)
Kindle Edition (amazon.com)

https://amzn.to/36WX3go

About Terry

Terry Toler is an Amazon international # 1 best-selling and award-winning author. He writes clean fiction with a message and life-changing nonfiction. He's a public speaker, entrepreneur, and has authored more than forty books.

Sign up for his newsletter where you'll get free stuff, exclusive content, and news of releases and promotions. He can be followed at terry-toler.com.

If you like his books, please take a few minutes to leave a review on Amazon. We really appreciate it. It helps draw more readers to his books. Thanks!

www.ingramcontent.com/pod-product-compliance
Lightning Source LLC
Chambersburg PA
CBHW020315260626
47156CB00004B/1229